LONELY LIONESS

THE LIONESS'S HAREM: BOOK ONE

CATHERINE BANKS

TURBO KITTEN

Thank you to these amazing people:
Pauline, you're always such a great help! I would be lost without you.
My husband and best friend, Avery. The moon of my life, and the
reason I am able to do what I love.
Michelle F. Your insights are always wonderful and your help is always
appreciated.
C.R., for all of your kind words, hard work, and optimism.
R.J. for your harsh love, which is totally needed, and all of your
teachings.
And, last but definitely not least, thank you to my BFF, Jenica. I love
you and I'm so glad we found each other.

CHAPTER ONE

FINDING A LION MATE WAS PROVING MUCH MORE DIFFICULT THAN I had planned. If I didn't find a male soon, I feared I might never. Okay, that was being dramatic. I was young still, but with my standards, I was worried I would never find a match. Or worse, be forced to settle.

The classroom was eerily quiet as Professor Cleo began reading. "Mighty Gilgamesh came on and Enkidu met him at the gate. He put out his foot and prevented Gilgamesh from entering the house, so they grappled, holding each other like bulls. They broke the doorposts and the walls shook, they snorted like bulls locked together. They shattered the doorposts and the walls shook. Gilgamesh bent his knee with his foot planted on the ground and with a turn Enkidu was thrown. Then immediately his fury died. When Enkidu was thrown he said to Gilgamesh, 'There is not another like you in the world. Ninsun, who is as strong as a wild ox in the byre, she was the mother who bore you, and now you are raised above all men, and Enlil has given you the kingship, for your strength surpasses the strength of men.' So Enkidu and Gilgamesh embraced and their friendship was sealed." Professor Cleo stopped reading and stared at the ground, letting the story sink in and letting us think about it. "Think on that this weekend."

I left the class feeling smarter and enlightened. I had known many who had gained friendship through similar battles. The day was warm and I inhaled the scents of the world around me. The leaves swayed on the gentle spring breeze, and students walked to and from classrooms. I made my way to the bus stop and sat down on one of the benches as I waited. It was a challenge to take college classes while still in high school, but I loved learning such rich information and being able to take whatever classes I wanted. A couple of girls sat down on the bench beside me and chatted about their holidays and how much they had missed each other. I let their chatter die into the background as I daydreamed about what my life would be like if I was human.

"Check him out," one of the girls whispered, drawing my attention back to them.

"Oh my God. He is hot!" a different girl whispered back.

I looked in the direction their eyes were locked and had to agree with them, the guy was attractive, but too weak for me. Any human would be too weak for me. I had learned from a very early age that guys did not like their girls stronger than them. They also did not like it when you were faster or better at sports than them either.

The bus pulled up in front of us, and we boarded it, showing the driver our passes and taking seats. I was lucky enough to have a bus that took me from my college to my high school.

My cell phone buzzed in my pocket and I sighed, already knowing it was a text message from my father. I pulled it out of my pocket and was shocked to see it was a text from Felix, a human boy I had befriended. I slid my finger across the screen to unlock it and responded to his text of, *"When will you be here?"*

Me: *On the bus now. Will be @ school in 20. Y?*

I waited nervously for his response. He would text me occasionally when he was bored, but our conversations had only been about how stupid the cheerleaders were or how much we hated high school. I had noticed an increase in his pheromones lately, but I was trying to ignore them and hope that he learned from my mannerisms that I was not interested in him.

My phone vibrated and a text of *"I'm bored"* popped up.

I exhaled a sigh of relief. I was not confident that I was out of hot water with him yet, but this was a positive sign. Me: *Picture the girls forming a pyramid and falling onto each other. That helps me.*

I got back the text of *"lol"* as I had predicted I would. I put my phone away and watched the city pass by. Tonight, was a family dinner, and I was dreading it immensely. My family was not your typical mother, father, and children who sat around the dinner table and talked about their day at work and school. My family consisted of an alpha werelion and his pride of five were-lionesses, me, and two other werelions. We were not lions, like the animals that run around in Africa, but a decedent of the *Smilodon fatalis* and *Smilodon populator* from prehistoric times with extra-long fangs called sabre teeth and bodies more like very large bobcats than lions. Most people referred to us as Sabre-toothed tigers when they saw us, but again, we were not tigers. I guess we were not easily classified as anything thanks to the magic that allowed us to transform. Don't ask me why we were called werelions when we weren't lions. I guess calling us weresmilodons was too weird sounding. The Smilodons often fought with the dire wolves back in prehistoric times, like we fought the werewolves who are their descendants now. Could our battles stem from prehistoric nature? Could it simply be a left over instinct to fight each other?

My mother was constantly fighting my father's other two mates and family dinners tended to end in my mother slamming one of their faces into a food dish. I was not sure why she did not just kill Lucy, my mother's nemesis and my father's favorite. I would not let another female take away the attention of my mate from me. I needed to talk to mom and ask her why she had not killed Lucy yet. There was probably some werelion code that forbade her from doing so, and if that were true, then I definitely needed to learn about it so I didn't get in trouble if I ended up killing one of my mate's other partners.

My mate. That had such a nice ring to it and yet sounded like a fantasy at the same time. Werelions were few and far between because they were always fighting with each other as well as werewolves and most did not live past twenty-two. I had been searching for a mate and was learning why werelionesses traveled a lot. In order to find a mate who you not only were attracted to, but also got along with, was a daunting task. I knew I was only seventeen, but every day I saw girls with their boyfriends or husbands and I felt this emptiness and jealousy so intense that sometimes I wanted to tear someone's head off. When would I meet my mate? *Would* I find a mate? Or would I have to settle for being someone's third or fourth mate?

It still shocked me that the males were allowed to have multiple female mates when there were far less females than males. We should have been the ones with our harem of males, not the other way around.

I heard growling in the back of the bus and turned around slowly, making eye contact with an ugly guy in his thirties. He was showing me his teeth and growling just loud enough for me to hear, but soft enough that the humans around us would not notice. I inhaled and resisted the urge to hiss at him. He was a male from the Canine Pack, a werewolf. In North America there were two main clans, the Canine Pack and the Feline Pride. When around each other, our clans tended to fight, and the battle ended up with one person very bloody and tired and another in pieces on the ground. The Feline Pride usually won because dogs are no match against lions, but there had been some inexperienced werelions who had lost to werewolves. Their main mistake was not changing forms. As humans we were almost evenly matched, but as animals, lions had the upper paw.

My stop came into view, but I kept my eyes on the werewolf. I had no clue if he was going to attack me simply for being a were-lion or if he was going to just show me his teeth to let me know that he was not scared of me. The bus stopped, and I showed him my teeth once before quickly exiting. I would have to remember to keep an eye out for him when I was at the college. I did not need to get attacked and have to explain to my dad why I had killed yet another werewolf.

It was not my fault that they felt the need to attack me. It was like they thought they had to prove something and since I was a seventeen-year-old girl they figured they had a chance of taking me out. I laughed to myself. I was not so easily taken down.

I made my way into the school, head held high.

"Hey, Ainsley," a soft female voice with a hint of an accent said from in front of me.

I looked up and smirked at Theresa, a tough as nails Latina, who had transferred to Sierra Oaks High School after getting in too many fights at the ghetto school Los Alamos. She was wearing blue jeans and a tank top, which allowed her to show off the tattoo on her upper arm and was letting her long, thick black hair hang down in luxurious waves behind her. It was the first time I had seen her hair down.

"Hey, Theresa. I like your hair," I said pleasantly without smiling. Sometimes when I smiled people freaked out. Dad said it's because they know that we were showing them our teeth, a sign of aggression usually, and are instinctively frightened. I am not sure if I believe him, but people do tend to take a step back when I smile at them sometimes.

The first day Theresa had come to school, she instinctively felt the need to move out of my way. The only problem was that she was used to being the tough girl on campus and so she had chosen to purposefully step *into* my way. I admired her bravery, no matter how stupid it was for a human to challenge a werelion, and had befriended her.

"How was class?" she asked as we walked towards third period math.

"It was great. I love listening to Professor Cleo read. She makes that class."

Theresa shook her head. "I don't understand you girls *wanting* to go to additional classes. I can't wait to get out of high school and move away from all of this."

It was a conversation we had had several times and no matter how I explained it to her, she did not understand it from my point of view. I shrugged. "Some of us actually like school."

"*Loca*," she said in her beautiful Spanish accent. "You girls are just *locas*."

"*Yo soy muy bonita*," I said in my best Spanish.

She laughed. "Yes, you are pretty. *¡Tu eres espantosa!*"

"I am not frightening," I said as I pretended to look hurt and sad.

She shook her head. "You don't trick me, *chica*. You remind me of this leopard I once saw at a zoo. You are calm and act innocent, but the moment someone's back is turned, you will strike out in hopes of getting something in our claws."

I tried to clear the image in my head because I had not yet changed and I was in desperate need of a little cat and mouse fun. It would be great to change right there in the middle of the quad and chase around the kids from my school. I wouldn't even kill them, but just the taste of their fear on my tongue and the sight of those preppy cheerleaders peeing themselves as I cornered them was enough to make me purr in delight and seriously consider it.

"Hey," Felix said as he met up with us. "What's up?" He had on his usual baggy jeans and large sweater. It seemed like he wore them to try to appear larger than he actually was.

"The sun," I said sarcastically.

"The stars," Theresa said.

Felix rolled his eyes. "Hilarious."

A group of five girls giggled at something one of them had said as they turned down a hallway to the left of us. Theresa, Felix and I watched them and then all of us rolled our eyes.

"You think one of them explained how two plus two actually equals four and the others realized how dumb they were to think it was five?" Theresa asked with venom in her voice.

In my little group we all had different reasons for disliking the cheerleaders. Theresa hated them because she thought they were pretty white girls who had it easy. Felix hated them because none of the girls would pay him any attention since he was a weakling. I hated them because they had no idea how easy it was for them. They had their choice of males whereas I may never find a male or if I did, he might already have three other mates and I would have to forever compete with them, like my mom had to, or he could be killed soon after I meet him. Mom did not understand why I befriended humans at the school, and I could not really explain it. Dad said he thought I had befriended them because Felix was so weak, I had a weird protective instinct and that Theresa was like a lion cub, fierce, very vulnerable, and likely to get herself in trouble.

Felix opened the door for us, and we took our seats in the center of the classroom, pulling out our math books and blank paper. Most students hated math, but I loved it. It was one of the few classes where I excelled. I took out my pencil and started doodling an image of a lion ripping off a wolf's head.

"Feeling a little morbid today?" Felix asked me.

I smiled and said, "Just thinking about this dream I had where I was a lion and had killed a wolf." I could still remember the taste of his blood and the way his body had looked once he was dead.

"Is a lion your favorite animal or something?" Theresa asked. "Because you sure talk about lions a lot."

"Yes, they are my favorite."

The bell rang, announcing the start of class, and I focused on the lesson at hand even though I already knew how to answer the problems. I helped Theresa and Felix with their problems and explained it to them as best as I could. As the bell rang, they both seemed to finally understand it. "I told you guys it wasn't that difficult."

"It's stupid," Felix said. "I'm never going to need to know this stuff later in life."

"Ainsley, can I talk to you?" a very attractive Chuck asked as he stepped away from his circle of jocks. Chuck had dark skin, the sexiest smile I had ever seen and an amazing body from hours of working out every day in the gym. He was the most wanted bachelor at school and he had a thing for me, but sadly I could only enjoy looking at him since he was, after all, only human.

"What's up, Chuck?" I asked in a cheery voice.

He laughed at me. "You just love saying that don't you?"

I shrugged. "What can I say? I'm easy to entertain."

"Are you busy tonight?" he asked.

If you count watching my mom fight with my dad's two other wives as being busy then, yes. "I sort of have a family thing. Why?"

He seemed seriously bummed. "Oh. Well, tonight's the last game, and I was hoping you would come watch."

I had forgotten that it was nearing the end of their football private league already. The state loved football so much that they had a second football season with private leagues that combined players from different high schools together.

"Oh. Well, I might be able to weasel my way out of the family thing, but my dad is pretty strict about me going," I said.

He smiled. "I would really like to see you there. It would definitely make me play better."

I pushed his arm gently with my fist, just enough to make his shoulder move. "And we all know you need as much help as you can get in that area."

"Burn!" Sean, one of the football players yelled, making the rest of Chuck's group laugh.

Chuck handed me a piece of paper with his phone number on it and said, "Text me later and let me know if you'll be able to make it."

"Sure thing," I said and then saluted him with the piece of paper. I walked over to my group, and we continued on our way to lunch, getting in line and then taking our tray of food outside to sit against the wall of one of the classroom buildings.

"What are your plans this weekend?" Theresa asked Felix.

He shrugged. "Play *World of Warcraft*."

"What time? I might get on tonight?" she said as she took a bite from her burger.

"You play *WoW*?" I asked in shock. It was a total nerd game and Theresa was anything but nerdy, or at least I had thought.

She smiled. "You don't know much about me, *chicka*. I love RPGs and MMORPGs."

I was completely lost. What the hell did those acronyms mean? "Cool," I said instead of commenting any further.

"What? You don't think I can be tough and be a gamer? I'll cut you if you say anything."

I believed her. I smiled, showing a little more teeth than I usually did with her. "You would try."

Felix stopped eating and looked at me with dilated pupils and sweat beginning to drip from his enlarged pores.

Theresa tried to meet my eyes, but she bowed her head to the side after a moment. "Right," she said with a smile, trying to lighten the atmosphere again.

"What are you going to do?" Felix asked me.

"I'm going on a weekend trip to go shopping." Shopping for *guys*. I bit my lip to keep from giggling.

"What are you shopping for?" Theresa asked.

"New clothes and Christmas presents," I answered automatically since it was the same excuse I had used on my dad. Speaking of my dad, I needed to text him and ask if I could stay for the football game tonight. Even if I could not date Chuck, I still liked flirting with him.

"Christmas shopping already?" Theresa asked. "Isn't it a little early?"

"It's only a couple of months away, and I have a lot of people to shop for." Even if I did not like my dad's other mates, I still had to buy them presents since my dad forced them to buy me presents, too. I sent my dad a text asking if I could stay after school and miss the family dinner and then continued eating my food. My stomach growled, not being even half full from the measly human portions that the school gave us.

"What are you doing this weekend?" Felix asked Theresa.

She shrugged. "Just hanging out at home. So, let me know if you get on *WoW* because otherwise my weekend will prove to be incredibly boring."

My phone vibrated in my pocket to let me know that a phone call was incoming. I answered without looking at the caller id. "Yello."

"Ainsley," Dad said. "What is the reason you want to stay after school?"

I could hear Stacy, Dad's other mate in the background giggling about something. She was always laughing about something.

"It's the last game of the season for the league and I'd like to go. It's good for me to experience high school like a normal kid, right?"

He growled, hating that I was using his own words against him. "Fine. Be home by eleven."

"Thanks, Dad," I said with a broad smile on my face.

"I better not smell any human boy's scents on you when you come home."

"That's gross, Dad. Seriously. I can't even believe you just said that to me."

He laughed. "That's my girl. Love you."

"Love you, too."

I hung up and texted Chuck to let him know that I would be at the game.

"Going to the game?" Theresa asked with a smirk on her face.

"Yes," I said. "Want to stay with me and hang out?"

"Sorry, *chica*, but I stay away from sports functions," she said as she tossed her empty food tray into the trashcan.

"I could go with you if you want someone to sit with you?" Felix offered.

I choked on the soda I was drinking and coughed for a full minute before being able to catch my breath. "Um…thanks Felix, but I'll be okay."

His eyebrows furrowed in frustration and he stood up, throwing away his food and putting his back pack on. "Fine. Whatever."

I watched him walk away and felt like I should say something, but I couldn't think of anything to say that would not make him think I was interested in him.

"He'll get over it. You just hurt his feelings."

"He has to know that I'm not interested in him, right?" I asked her.

She laughed. "In a guy's mind if you talk to them then they have a chance."

I groaned. "That is so stupid."

The bell rang announcing the end of the lunch period. "Let me know how tonight goes. And watch your back. Those cheer-leaders do not like that Chuck pays attention to you instead of them."

I always watched my back. "Thanks," I said as I watched her head off towards her last period. I started walking towards my fourth period when I received a text from Chuck. I stepped out of the way of the flow of traffic to read the message.

"Glad you'll be able to make it. I'll look for you in the stands."

I wished I had a werelion I could flirt with like this. Thinking about it made my chest hurt and made me feel so incredibly alone that I almost whined out loud. Most thought it was stupid for teenagers to feel alone just because they did not have a boyfriend, but for pack animals, like me, we craved others to be around. Yes, I had a lot of other werelionesses around me, but I did not like most of them and they did not like me. Someday I hoped to find a Pride that I felt accepted in, not one that I was born into and stuck with until I found a mate and joined his Pride.

"Earth to Ainsley, get to class," Mr. Smith said from in front of me.

I looked up and asked, "Do I have to?"

He smiled. "Sadly yes, but at least today is Friday."

I put my phone away and headed towards class. "Fine then. I guess I will suffer through Ms. Dallas' boring lecture on history."

"Just be happy it's a short schedule because of the pep rally," he called, "Or she might go off on a story about her childhood."

I laughed and started walking backwards so I could see him as I talked. "I do like hearing about how she tamed dinosaurs though."

He laughed and then wagged his finger at me. "That's mean."

I went to class and spaced out during the lecture because I hated history. I wished they would tell the true story of the world. The story that involved the paranormal world and how we had to remain hidden because humans were fearful beings that hated anything not like them. If the paranormals could rule, then I would be able to see Pegasi fly and talk with dragons and I wouldn't have to hear about the stupid human wars over dinosaur bones and land. It wasn't Native Americans whose land was taken away, but shapeshifters. Most of them had been wiped out and now only the wereanimals were left in the shifters categories and very few of us at that. The humans had slowly been killing us off or breeding our paranormal abilities out of us. If I had one wish, I would give up a mate to have paranormals free to walk about as they pleased.

The bell rang, and I made my way to the gymnasium with the rest of the kids to sit through the pep rally. It was my last year of high school and I decided that I should at least be slightly engaged in school activities. The football players ran into the gymnasium and the school erupted in cheers. I clapped along with them and whistled when they announced Chuck's name. Camille, the head cheerleader and the one girl who absolutely and unconditionally hated me, glared at me and whispered harshly to the other cheerleaders.

I smiled sweetly at her while envisioning chasing her down in a forest and listening to her frightened screams. The pep rally finally ended and we all made our way out to the football stadium. I paid my admission, purchased popcorn, soda and some candy and then found a seat. The junior varsity team played first and I cheered like a football crazy girl. I scoped out the opposing school on the other side of the stadium, but sadly there were no super attractive guys. I felt bad for the girls over there and wondered if they were all wishing for Chuck's attention as well.

My phone rang, and I answered it, despite the loud noise around me, I had excellent hearing so I could hear the other person's very well. "Hello?"

"Where are you?" Mom asked angrily.

"At a football game. Dad said I could," I said defensively.

"Of course he did. I can't believe you left me alone with these people."

"Mom, you are going to be alone with them as soon as I turn eighteen. I already told you that I am going to leave and search for a mate." She was so dramatic sometimes.

"Whatever. When will you be home?" she asked softer. I could hear someone enter her room and shut the door.

I held down the dry heave and said, "Eleven. I'll let you go so you can deal with your visitor."

"Bye, Ainsley," Dad said in the background.

I hung up before I could hear anything else. Ew. Parents were so gross. I focused on the junior varsity game and stood up and screamed in victory when we beat the other school, fourteen to zero. I went back to the snack shed and bought two hot dogs, two pretzels with cheese and three sodas. I hoped no one noticed that I ate them all myself. I did not need rumors being spread around that I was bulimic or something like that.

The varsity teams came out and I cheered with everyone, chanting our school's name over and over again. Chuck looked up in the stands and made eye contact with me, smiling wide and then winking at me. Camille followed his line of sight until she found me. Her eyebrows furrowed and I could practically see the steam coming out of her ears. I thought her head might explode.

The crowd sat down, and the game began. I had never really paid attention to sports before so I was not completely sure what was happening, but I understood when our team made it to the end of the field and scored a goal, or touchdown as the announcer said. Part of me longed to be able to compete, but I knew the reasons my dad forbade me from sports was because I would be too good at it and I would get noticed for my super human strength and speed.

I finished my food as discreetly as possible and walked to the nearest trashcan to throw my garbage away. As I headed back towards my seat I caught the slightest scent of a wolf. I turned around slowly, searching for the owner of the scent, but I couldn't find anyone who looked likely to be a wolf. Had I imagined it? Possibly. The run in with the wolf on the bus must have jarred my nerves more than I realized.

I watched the game, but paid more attention to my surroundings to ensure that I did not get snuck up on. Unfortunately, I lost my enjoyment of the game because I was not focused on it. As the game ended and we stood up to sing the alma mater, the hair on the back of my neck stood up and I felt someone watching me. I could not stay and talk to Chuck. I needed to get out of here, now. I hurried out of the stadium, weaving my way in and out of people, trying to keep from touching anyone. I had not felt this nervous in a very long time and I did not like it. I drove home as quickly as possible, needing the security of my pride around me.

I drove away from the city and out into the rural area. Most of the rural area was flat, open grassland, but the twenty acres my dad owned was dense with trees. So dense that it looked like a mini forest in the middle of the fields. It reminded me of video games where you looked at a map and most of it was open land and there was one spot that was a thick, dense forest, usually called The Forest of Death or something like that. Our property was also fenced with very thick bars and spikes at the top that made it impossible for humans to climb. The spikes were tipped with silver to keep werewolves out as well.

I stopped at the gate keypad and typed in my code. The gate opened silently, and I hurried down the long driveway to the main house. Dad had three houses on the property. The main house was where everyone came for family meals and where he and his mates lived. The other two houses were for the other werelions so that they were separated from Dad's mates. Even though he allowed them to be part of the pride, he still made sure to keep his mates away from the other males. He was very protective. I lived in the main house with him, but by June I would be moving away.

I parked my nineteen sixty five Ford Mustang and hurried up to the house. Even though I knew no one had followed me, I still felt uneasy and wanted to get inside and near my dad as soon as possible.

I reached for the door knob, but my mom opened the door before I could turn it. "It's about time you got home," she hissed.

"Nice to see you, too," I grumbled as I walked past her and into the living room where everyone was sitting together. Despite how childish it was and that I knew mom would tease me for it later, I walked to my dad and sat on the floor at his feet, leaning my head against his knee to inhale his scent and try to calm my nerves.

"Everyone leave," Dad said calmly as he pet my hair.

"What?" my mom asked in shock.

"Leave. I need to speak with my daughter," he said.

I froze under his touch, unsure why he wanted to talk to me. Had I done something wrong? Everyone left without another word and as soon as we heard all of their bedroom doors shut, my dad climbed down on the floor beside me and looked into my eyes. "What's wrong? Did something happen?"

I had forgotten about my dad's alpha instincts. He could probably sense my nervousness. "It's nothing. I just felt like I was being watched and couldn't shake the feeling."

"You're not usually so easily rattled," he commented. "Did something happen earlier?"

I sighed. I hated that he was so intuitive. "Nothing I could not handle myself. I just saw a wolf on the bus and he growled at me."

"Did he touch you?" he asked as his eyes changed from their normal human blue to a lion's amber.

I smirked at him, giving him my best cocky look. "Of course not. And if he had, I would have ripped his arm off."

He smiled at me and ruffled my hair. "That's my girl. You know if you need me for anything, you can always call. I will come to you for whatever you need."

I rubbed my head against his hand and purred. "Thanks Dad."

"Love ya, kiddo."

I smiled and threw my body sideways, knocking him over. "You old softy."

He grabbed me and pinned me against his body. "Not as soft as you think," he said and then licked my face.

"Dad!" I groaned. "No licking."

He laughed and then released me. "Go to bed. You've got a long day ahead of you tomorrow."

"Can I borrow some money?" I asked him. "I have my savings, but I would like to get presents for my two human friends at school in addition to everyone in the pride."

He sighed as he pulled his wallet out of his back pocket. "You women are going to drain my bank account faster than my patience."

I laughed. "That's your own fault for taking so many mates."

He growled. "Don't remind me."

"Dad," I asked, "Do you think it's possible for a lion to have only one mate?"

He closed his wallet and said, "Some males only take one mate because they can't handle defending more than one, but in the back of their mind they always hope for more. Some males only take one because they are too lazy to search for more, but again if they come across another they would probably add her to their pride. Most males take several mates though because we can protect them all, and it proves how strong we really are. Besides, what type of pride could one have if it consisted of only one female? Who would hurt and how could the alpha be sure that his mate was not sleeping with the other males?"

I let everything he said sink in and felt my hopes dwindling. I wished for a mate who would only need me, but he was right. It would be a pathetic pride if it only consisted of two. "The alpha would have to trust his mate, I guess," I responded.

"Sweetheart, I know it's not ideal for humans, but you are not human. You are a werelioness and you crave being in a large pride. Could you imagine only living with one other person and only hunting with one other lion?"

"I'm going to rip out your throat!" Mom yelled at someone.

"It would be a lot quieter," I said.

Dad laughed and stood up, holding his hand out to me. "Yes,

that it would. Here," he said and handed me three hundred dollars. "Try to be frugal."

I hugged him and then kissed his cheek. "Thanks, Dad. You're the best."

He headed down the hallway towards the sounds of fighting. "I know, sweetheart. I know."

CHAPTER TWO

THE DRIVE TO THE BEACH WAS ONLY ABOUT AN HOUR, BUT ONCE you hit the traffic it ended up being an hour and a half due to all of the people trying to get their last bit of warm time fun in before the winter came. I parked my car in one of the many parking garages and made my way down to the beach. Luckily it was warm enough to wear my shortest shorts and a tank top that hugged my body. I held my flip flops in my hand as I walked along the beach, letting the still cool sand squished between my toes. It was only eight thirty in the morning so the sand was not yet warm from the sun. My plan was to walk along the beach for a while, go shop for my Christmas presents, put the presents in the car, walk along the beach some more and then go to a restaurant before heading home. I hoped that I might be able to at least meet a werelion during the day out here. My state had the third largest population of werelions in the country so I just had to keep my fingers crossed that one would be out here trying to have a day of fun in the sun.

I walked closer to the water, letting the waves roll over my feet. I shivered at the coldness, but the sun was beginning to warm my face so it wasn't unbearable. I loved the water and would have gone into the ocean if it weren't for my plan for the rest of the day.

A couple surfers were heading out into the water, and I checked them out as they checked me out. I inhaled, but sadly they were humans. I sneezed and rubbed my nose. Stupid salt.

"Not from around here are you?" a voice asked from behind me.

I turned slowly and smiled at the woman who looked to be in her early twenties walking beside me now. Werelioness. "I'm from inland," I said and then held out a hand. "Ainsley."

She shook it. "Sheila. You a wanderer?"

I shook my head. "Just enjoying the beach and then shopping."

She nodded. "We have great shopping here."

"We cool?" I asked her. It was always polite to get the permission of the local pride to hang out on their territory.

She smiled. "Of course. You're welcome to come back anytime. In fact, why don't you come meet my pride and have dinner?"

I had met other prides before when traveling with dad, but I had never gone to another pride without my dad. She noticed my hesitation and said, "I promise no harm will come to you and you will be free to leave whenever you want." She leaned closer and whispered, "We have single males."

I smiled at her and said, "You had me at 'no harm.'"

She laughed and said, "I like you, Ainsley. Meet me at pier seven at six o'clock and I'll have you follow me out to our place. Cool?"

"Cool," I said with a nod of my head.

"Later," she said with a wave and then jogged down the beach. I watched her go and felt happy that I was going to get to meet another pride and some single males. I knew today would be productive. I made my way to the stores and started the daunting task of buying Christmas presents for my pride and my two human friends. I bought my mom a new shiny purse and dad a new wallet that had drawings of money flying away. I bought Lucy a bottle of perfume that smelled like roses, her favorite scent and I bought Stacy a Coach scarf that matched the new purse she had just purchased last month.

I could not pick a gift for Theresa or Felix from the stores that were around there, so I took what I had purchased and headed down to the car, locking everything inside the trunk. I checked my watch and was pleased to see that I had finished with an hour to spare until I had to meet Sheila. I decided to call my dad and tell him what I was doing. I had to make sure that he knew where I was just in case something bad happened so he would be able to come take revenge.

"Hello, Ainsley," Dad said with a yawn.

"Hey, Dad. I was invited by the local pride to eat dinner with them. I'll text you the address once I get it. Okay?"

He growled into the phone. "You be careful and keep your guard up at all times. If I don't hear back from you by eleven o'clock I will personally come down there and rip off every one of their heads."

I smiled at his very serious threat. "I promise I will call by eleven."

"Good girl. Have fun and tell Marcus, if he is still their alpha, that I said 'hello.'"

"Yes, sir. Tell mom what I'm doing, okay?"

"Okay. Bye."

I hung up the phone and drove my car down to the pier where I was supposed to meet Sheila. She wasn't there yet so I bought an ice cream cone from one of the vendors on the street and watched the waves rolling in and out.

"It's beautiful, isn't it?" Sheila asked.

She was very stealthy, but I had heard her four feet away from me. "Yeah, I could definitely live down here," I said longingly, "But sadly I don't think that is in the cards for me."

"Well, let's head out. I let our Alpha know you were coming and he said he is delighted and is making a dinner for your visit."

"That's so nice," I said, genuinely shocked by the act of kindness. She climbed into a cute little Honda, and I followed behind her in my Mustang. We drove for about thirty minutes along the shoreline and then headed inland for five minutes. Sheila stopped in front of fifteen foot gates made of metal and honked her horn three times. The massive gates opened and she drove inside. I marked the address in my phone and sent my dad a text message with its location. One could never be too safe.

We drove down a driveway of gravel into a hidden jungle paradise. "Wow," I whispered as we parked in front of a mansion with large werelion sculptures on either side of the entrance. I climbed out of the car and was greeted by a young werelion boy no older than eight running out to my car.

"Hi. I'm Joseph. What's your name?" he asked with a smile.

"I'm Ainsley," I said.

"Joseph, that is no way to greet a guest," a commanding male's voice said from the doorway of the mansion. I turned and met his eyes, holding his gaze for a full minute before looking down. "Hello Ainsley," he said and smiled at me. "How is your father?"

"He is doing great. He said to tell you 'hello,'" I said with a smile back to him.

"Please, come inside," he said with a sweep of his arm. "You are always welcome in our territory."

"Thank you," I said as I shut my door and followed him inside. The living room was large and exquisitely decorated. "Your place is beautiful," I whispered.

"Thank you," he said with a bow of his head. "Dinner is ready and waiting for you," he said as he pushed open a double set of doors, leading me into a large formal dining room.

My nose was instantly filled with the scents of six females, one being Sheila, and five males. Marcus stepped to the side so the room could see me and said, "This is Ainsley, a visitor from the pride up north and inland. Her father and I go very far back and I do not want to have to fight him last time did not end very well for either of us. So, please treat her with respect and if any of you harms her without due cause, I will personally rip out your throats." The group sat eerily still as the threat sunk in. "Now, let's eat." He said with a cheery attitude.

I sat down in an open chair beside Sheila and right across from two very attractive teenage males. The table was filled with several types of meat, including deer and duck as well as two pasta dishes. The alpha made his plate, and then everyone else started digging in. I filled up my plate and ate as I listened to the pleasant conversations and funny stories. Was this pride always like this? Or were they just on their best behavior and not fighting because I was here? Marcus' mates seemed to be getting along well and smiling though, not even like they were playing. Was it possible? Were other prides actually pleasant at shared dinners?

When everyone had finished eating, Marcus sent everyone out to the backyard to enjoy desert. I followed behind Sheila and one of the teenagers walked beside me. "Hi, I'm Jason."

"Nice to meet you, Jason," I said with a smile. He was very cute, but not very dominant. I knew I could not really be picky, but there had to be a male more dominant than him that I could find as a mate.

"So, are you looking for a mate?" he asked.

Wow, straight to the point. "Yes, I am actually."

"Well, Max and Iagan are the two single males," he said.

I looked at him curiously. "What about you?"

He smiled. "I'm only thirteen."

I gasped. "Oh my god you look like you are at least seventeen." Werelions aged slowly once they reached thirty. In fact most looked thirty until they were in their seventies. Werelionesses aged slowly as well, but we did not slow down in our aging until our forties.

He beamed proudly. "Thanks. Besides, we both know you weren't interested in me anyways."

How did he know? "No offense, but I'm glad now that I know how old you are."

He laughed. "I get that a lot."

"Do you guys get a lot of females coming here?" I asked him curiously.

He shrugged. "We get an occasional traveler, but most are in their twenties." He led me over to a set of outdoors couches. "Max, Iagan, this is Ainsley."

Max stood up and held out his hand to me. "It's nice to meet you, Ainsley." I shook his hand and he inhaled my scent deeply, a sign that he was interested in me.

"Nice to meet you as well, Max."

Iagan stood up and shook my hand with a sexy smirk on his face. "Hello, Ainsley." He inhaled my scent as well and held my hand for a moment longer than was normal protocol.

"Hi, Iagan."

For a moment everyone simply stood still, me looking at each of the free males and them staring straight at me. Max was more handsome than Iagan, but Iagan had a better body and a few tattoos that added to his hotness factor. They were both dominant enough to be alphas and judging by their bodies, I would bet a fight between them would be a very close battle.

"Let's sit and enjoy dessert," Sheila said as she set a tray of cookies on the table in between the couches. I sat down on the couch opposite Iagan and Max and reached for a cookie before either could offer one to me.

"Your place is gorgeous. I bet it's great to be able to change and imagine that you are running through the jungle," I said longingly.

"You should stay the night and go on a midnight run with us," Iagan offered. "The moonlight shines down through the canopy just like in the real jungle.

"Could she stay overnight?" Sheila asked Marcus who was walking outside with a tray of milk glasses. "It's been so long since I've had a female my age to spend time with."

Marcus set the tray down and pet her hair. "That is up to Ainsley. I give my permission though."

"Will you?" Sheila asked me hopefully.

They seemed nice enough and I could not sense hostility from any of them. Since Marcus was so much older than me, I doubted that his mates would think I was any competition. "I have to check with my alpha, but I would love to."

Sheila smiled happily and handed me a glass of milk. "I hope he says yes. It sucks being the only teenage girl sometimes."

I took a bite from my cookie and moaned. "This is amazing."

"Max bakes them," Sheila said with a smirk.

"I like baking," he said defensively.

"It's delicious," I told him honestly. I did not want to tell him that chocolate chip cookies were my favorite cookies.

"So how many are in your pride?" Max asked.

Marcus smacked the back of his head. "It is impolite to ask about the strength of one's pride."

Max cringed. "Sorry, alpha."

I smiled. "It's alright. I know your pride is allied with mine."

"True," Marcus said.

"My pride consists of the alpha, his three mates, two werelions and me," I answered. It was a decent sized pride and the fact that we had two werelions in our pride was a sign of a powerful alpha. Or a stupid alpha if he allowed males who were stronger than him into the pride and they ended up stealing his mates.

"Do you go to school with the humans?" Sheila asked.

I nodded. "I go to high school locally and am taking a college class in addition."

"College?" Max asked. "Really?"

I nodded. "I wanted to get a head start on my college education." I was not sure when I would be able to truly start college because of my need to travel in search of a mate. Could I take Max or Iagan as a mate?

"How old are you?" Sheila asked.

"Seventeen," I said. "I turn eighteen in June."

She whistled. "I thought you were nineteen at least."

You age a lot when you have been through as much stuff as I have. "Thanks," I said with a laugh, trying to stave off the painful memories.

"Would you like another cookie?" Max asked.

"Thanks, but I think I'm going to call my alpha and make sure he is okay with me staying the night." I stood up and Max and Iagan stood up with me. That was a definite bonus for them. I liked a man with manners.

I walked through the mansion and out to the front driveway as I dialed my dad.

"Ainsley," Dad said softly. "How is it going?"

"Well," I answered. "One of the females here is my age and asked if I could stay the night to go on a midnight hunt with them."

Dad was eerily silent for at least two minutes before he finally asked, "Do you trust them?"

"Marcus is still alpha here and threatened to kill anyone who harmed me," I assured him.

Dad laughed. "Alright, I trust Marcus enough, but remember—"

"Watch my back," I finished for him.

"That's my girl. Call me in the morning."

"Yes, sir," I said and then hung up the phone. I smelled Iagan approaching and kept facing forward. "You're not very stealthy, sneaking up on a girl when she can smell you a mile away."

"If I was trying to sneak up on you I wouldn't do it in my human form," he said as he circled around to my front. "So, what did your alpha say?"

"He said I could stay."

"Great," he said with a smile. "I can't wait to see you in your lioness form."

I walked towards the mansion, looking back at him and said, "I usually make a guy buy me dinner first, but since your pride fed me, I guess I'll let it slide this time."

He laughed and followed me inside. Marcus and the rest of the pride were still in the back so I walked out to them. "He said I could stay the night," I said to Sheila who smiled happily.

Marcus smiled, too. "Great. Sheila will show you to your room where you can change. We will wait downstairs for you."

Sheila hopped up and put her arm around my shoulders as she led me upstairs. "I'm so excited. It's been so long since I've had a girl my age around here."

I smiled at her. "It's been a long time since I've had a girl my age as well. The youngest female in my pride is thirty-two."

"I feel your pain," she said. She stopped in front of the fourth door down and said, "Here is one of our guest rooms. You can use it. The handles on the inside of the door are long enough that you should be able to push it down with one of your paws and get out. If you can't though, just roar, and I'll come let you out."

"Thanks," I said as I walked inside and shut the door. I started stripping out of my clothes immediately, folded them and laid them on the large four poster bed. Everything in this house was so exquisite and beautiful that it made me a little jealous. We were not poor, but we were not rich like this pride.

I shoved away the thoughts and dropped down to my hands and knees to shift. I could shift in any position, but it was the least painful when shifting while on my hands and knees. I focused on the positive, the fact that I had found two free males and both were interested in me. And that I might have made a friend who was a werelioness like me. My body stretched taut, my pores expanded as fur began to grow through, and then in a strange magic pop, I was in my favorite form. I stretched my legs and walked around the room a couple of times to get used to being on four feet instead of two and then looked at myself in the mirror to the right of the bed.

The top of my head was five feet from the ground, my body weighed around four hundred pounds, and my sabre-teeth were a full foot long. My body was shaped similar to that of a bobcat, a very very large bobcat. My fur was similar to a snow leopard's, white fur and brown spots, but there were varying colorations around the world. I was excited to see what Max and Iagan looked like. I was small because I was young and female. Most full-grown males, like my father, weighed upwards of seven hundred pounds. Due to our sabre teeth we were not made for biting and pulling down our opponents or prey. Instead, we brought them down with our massive paws, subduing them with our weight and then delivering the killing bite to the jugular.

I lifted my lips in a snarl, pleased with my ferocious look, and purred at my reflection. I walked over to the door and smacked the long straight door handle with my paw, opening the door easily and headed down stairs. I could not hear anyone inside so I headed out back, following the scent trail that Sheila had left. I followed the trail passed the couches, out into the trees and to a small clearing where the entire pride was gathered in their lion forms. I approached slowly, stepping on a couple of twigs to announce my arrival. All eyes turned to me and it took me all of thirty seconds to differentiate the animal forms in front of me with their human forms.

Max was very near my size, which was not a good sign for him. He did have beautiful chocolate brown fur, but I needed a male capable of protecting me, not one a similar size to me. He looked over my body, sizing me up.

I looked at Iagan whose size shocked me. He was almost as big as my dad and nearly as big as Marcus. He had similar coloring to me, except he had green eyes instead of my golden brown eyes. It made him look exotic and was very appealing, especially when combined with his size.

Sheila was an almost identical duplicate of me. She was the same size, same color and would have been my doppelganger if it had not been for the fact that I had a large black stripe across my chest from an old scar from a battle with a werewolf. I envied her unmarred chest and wished I had not fought with that wolf five years ago.

Marcus was still the largest and he nodded at me to let me know it was time to start. I ran in the middle of the pack, between Iagan and Max and we headed deep into their man-made jungle. I inhaled the smells of the jungle and decided I liked it. Even though I was raised in the forest, the jungle called to the primal side of me. How could it be so different from the forest? They were both large areas of thick trees?

Something big dashed across the path in front of us, running for all it was worth. Marcus roared and our pursuit began. I breathed in the scents of the lions around me and let the thrill of the chase increase my adrenaline. It had been a long time since I had gone on a hunt and I was enjoying myself.

The deer came into view and Marcus leapt onto its back while the rest of us latched onto the deer with our claws. After it was firmly secured to the ground with all of our weight, Marcus bit into its neck, killing it. I stepped back from the kill, separating myself from the pride so as not to interfere with their pecking order and eating rights. I laid down twenty feet away and watched them. No one attacked each other or even snarled as they ate. It was as though they all actually got along, even Marcus' mates. I wished my pride were like this.

Max and Iagan each brought me a piece of meat and I stared at them in shock. It was way too early for me to decide which one of them I liked and way too early to accept food from either of them. What was protocol? Had mom talked to me about a situation like this happening? I racked my brain, but could not remember.

Sheila came over to me and touched her nose to my forehead,

activating a telepathic link with me. *"If you eat a bite from each of the pieces they brought you then it will show that you are interested, but that you haven't decided yet. If you do not eat from either it will mean you are not interested in either as a mate."*

"Thanks."

I stood up and took a small bite from each of their pieces and then playfully swiped at Sheila who roared and ran after me, chasing me around the jungle. I climbed up trees and leapt from branch to branch as she followed me. It was thrilling and the most fun I had had in years. I was definitely going to need to come visit her often to play like this.

Her paw caught my back leg and I fell from the branch I was on, down to the ground on my feet. I spun around and started chasing her, playing our version of tag. Max started running beside me so I smacked him in the shoulder instead, making him "it" and then ran to the right, putting Iagan between Max and me. Max tried to get Iagan, but Iagan was too fast and easily dodged his attempts. Max finally hit Joseph with his paw and Joseph chased after me. Joseph was quick and almost touched me when Iagan leapt between us and took the hit for me. I would have thanked him, except that then he turned and started chasing me. I dashed around a few trees and then climbed up one, clinging to the trees with my claws and propelling myself up with my massive back leg muscles.

I made it to a branch fifteen feet off the ground and looked back down to find Iagan circling underneath me. *"You have to come down eventually,"* he said telepathically.

I almost lost my footing at having heard his voice in my head. We were not supposed to be able to communicate telepathically unless we were part of the same pride or if we had previously established a link, like Sheila had with me. I had not established a link with him, so how was he able to communicate with me?

"You really don't remember me, do you?" he asked and stopped pacing. *"I have to admit, that hurts my feelings a little."*

"*We've met before? Where?*" I asked, incredibly curious now. There were very few werelions that I forgot.

He huffed and said, "*Come down here and I will tell you.*"

I climbed down, and he smacked my shoulder with his paw. "*You're it!*"

"*You crafty jerk.*" I chased after him, roaring my fake anger and he ran as fast as he could, dodging my swipes and using the trees to keep just out of my reach. This was his home turf, and he was using every advantage that he could to stay away from my paws. I turned away from him, and tagged Max because he was just watching us and I realized I was focusing too much on one male, even if it was bothering the crap out of me that I had met him somewhere before and could not remember where.

We played for a few hours until I eventually fell in a heap. I looked at Sheila. "*I'm exhausted. I think I'm going to head off to sleep.*"

"*I think I'm ready for bed as well.*"

"*Goodnight, Ainsley,*" Iagan said. "*We can talk tomorrow.*"

I had no way of knowing if he was communicating on a level where Sheila could hear him or not, so I simply glared at him once and walked towards the house with Sheila beside me. I needed to talk to him so I could figure out how he knew me, but it would have to wait until tomorrow. I walked up the stairs, into the room they had assigned me, leaving the door slightly ajar and changed forms. It was quick and felt like a very good chill. I got dressed and listened to ensure that everyone came into the house. After about thirty minutes the house went quiet and I made my way out of the room and outside. I had left the door slightly open so that I could exit without anyone hearing me.

I walked out to the trees and found one very tall tree with very high branches and climbed up it. Once I felt that I was high enough to be safe, I lay down on my stomach on the branch, letting my arms and legs dangle downwards. It wasn't that I didn't trust the pride specifically, but I did not trust anyone except for my dad. I took a deep breath of the jungle air, tinged with a hint of sea water and fell into a deep sleep.

"You like sleeping in trees versus beds?" Iagan asked from very close to me.

I leapt up, balancing on my toes on the tree branch and snarled at him. What time was it? Why was he waking me up?

He was balanced on the end of my branch, squatted down on his toes with a relaxed look on his face. He raised his hands up, slowly to show he meant no harm and said, "I didn't mean to scare ̲you," he whispered. "I thought you had smelled me approach." He smirked. "You said my name so I thought you were awake."

I did not recall saying his name, but he didn't seem to be lying about that fact. How embarrassing. "I did not say your name," I said as I tried to compose myself. The sun was up so it was probably time for me to wake up anyways.

He stood and started walking towards me. "Why did you sleep in the tree?" he asked.

"I like trees," I answered as I stretched my arms up over my head.

"I like you," he whispered in a husky voice. "I haven't been able to stop thinking about you."

I dropped my arms and met his gaze. "You really know me?" I asked, shocked. "When did we meet?"

He looked sincerely hurt. "You really don't remember me?" he asked in a whisper. He shook his head and walked around me to lean a hand against the trunk of the tree and bow his head. "I suppose you could have suppressed that memory." He nodded his head. "That would make sense."

I growled in frustration. "Will you please tell me what you are talking about? I'm not trying to be rude, Iagan. I just don't remember ever meeting you before." Although something about him was starting to seem familiar.

"Well it was about five years ago," he said as he jumped from the branch we were on to a lower branch. "I was traveling around, trying to find a pride to take me in and while I was walking down the sidewalk of a pretty empty town, I heard the sounds of hissing and growling."

I followed him down the tree, listening to his story and feeling like I knew where this was going, yet I could not figure it out on my own.

"I followed the sounds into the mouth of an alley and stumbled upon the scent of a werelion and the scent of a werewolf. It wasn't any of my concern, but I just did not feel right leaving a fellow lion to fight a wolf alone. The farther down the alley I went, the louder the sounds of the fighting. I took two more steps and then I saw the craziest thing."

"What was it?" I asked, completely enrapt in his story telling.

"There was a girl, eleven or twelve years old, fighting with a fully grown, adult man. If it weren't for the scents and the eyes of both glowing in the dark, I would not have known they were anything other than human. At least that is what I thought until I saw the girl move. She moved like a well-trained assassin, darting in and hitting the man and ducking and dodging whenever the man tried to hit her. I stood like an idiot, watching the two fight before I realized that the girl was injured and even though she was indeed trained to fight, she was losing."

My brain began to formulate a memory from the recesses of my subconscious. Something that I had thought was only a dream, yet Iagan was replaying it for me.

"I leapt in without thinking and fought with the girl against the man, forcing him to retreat and leave the girl alone. I tried to talk to the girl, but she fled with terror in her eyes before I could even speak to her." He stopped walking, turning around to face me and said, "That was the last time I had seen you until yesterday when you walked into my house."

I stared into his eyes and felt myself drawn to him. I took a step back from him and whispered, "I'm sorry I ran away from you," I said, feeling incredibly embarrassed that I had done that. Still, why had a link been created? It didn't make sense. Unless... I'd done it during the fight to help ensure I didn't hurt him and only the man.

"It was understandable. You were young, injured and frightened, and I was a strange lion," he said as he took a step towards me.

I held my ground and kept our gazes even. "Thank you for helping me."

He lifted his hand and reached out towards me. I expected him to touch my face, but he placed his hand on my upper chest, where my scar was hidden underneath my shirt, and whispered, "I would do it again, in a heartbeat."

My heart sped up at his touch and the scent of him so close to me. How had I not remembered him? I should have at least remembered his scent.

Iagan leaned towards me and was about to kiss me when Max came into view and said, "There you two are! It's breakfast time."

I stepped back from Iagan, and smiled at Max. "Thanks. I'm starving."

"Sleeping in trees tends to make you hungry," Iagan whispered only loud enough for me to hear.

I looked at the smirk on his face and rolled my eyes at him. "What's for breakfast?" I asked Max as I walked passed him and towards the mansion.

"Steak and eggs," he answered from behind me.

I walked into the mansion, and Sheila put her arm around my shoulders, pulling me away from the guys. "I wondered where you went off to, but I can see now."

I rolled my eyes at her. "It wasn't like that."

She winked at me. "Sure."

I sat down and ate with everyone and once I was finished I stood up and faced Marcus. "Thank you for your hospitality. I will be sure to let my alpha know."

"You are always welcome here," He said with a smile. "I know Sheila will want to stay in touch with you."

"I'm sure I will come to visit soon," I said with a smile in return to him. I headed towards the door, waiting for Sheila to meet me. I held out my hand for her phone and typed in my contact information and then hit the call button. As soon as my phone vibrated and showed her number, I ended the call and handed her her phone back. "I would invite you to my place, but it sucks," I said with a laugh.

"Maybe you can come back in a couple weeks," she suggested. She looked at Max and Iagan who were waiting outside and said, "I know those two will want you to come back."

I smiled. "I'm sure my alpha will be okay with that. Text me."

She nodded. "Sure thing."

I walked out to my car which both Iagan and Max were leaning against. Max walked up to me and ran a hand through his hair sighing. "I really wish I had a chance with you because you are super hot, but I can tell that you and Iagan have a connection somehow."

"I'll keep you in mind if things don't work out," I said somewhat seriously.

He smiled. "Sweet."

I watched him walk away and felt weird. I knew that I should not let any single male leave before I actually gave them a chance, but knowing that Iagan was my savior and seeing how sexy he was, totally gave him an advantage.

"So, are you going to run away from me again?" he asked with his hands in his pockets.

I laughed and shook my head. "No, but I do need to head home."

He took my cellphone which was still in my hand and added his number and email to my contacts list and then added my info to his phone. "Will you call me when you get home so that I know you got there safely?"

"I can take care of myself," I said irritated.

He smiled. "I know that, Ainsley. It does not change the fact that I would like to know that you made it home safe."

"Why?" I asked softly. It was normal for a male to be protective of a female, but I felt like there was something deeper going on with him.

"I told you. I have not stopped thinking about you since that night. I have searched for you and now that I have found you, I do not want to lose you again. I want to get to know you and I want to give us a chance."

I leaned closer to him, purring and said, "Good answer." I climbed into my car and looked at him out my window, "I'll call you when I get home." It was an admission of my interest in him and the start of our relationship.

He smiled at me and said, "I'll keep my phone with me."

I drove away, looking at his reflection in the mirror and feeling hope for the first time in a long time. I could not believe I had lucked out this much! Not only had I found a free male, one who did not have any other mates, but he was very dominant, large, and had already proven that he could protect me once. I called my dad and let him know I was on my way home and sang along to the radio at the top of my voice, enjoying my happiness.

The drive took a while, and when I finally got home, I was bombarded by my mom and dad who sniffed me all over, memorizing the scents of those who had been around me, just in case they needed to go find them.

"Hi," I said as they stepped away from me. "I'm fine. They were very hospitable and treated me with respect."

"Good," dad said. "Did you finish shopping?"

In more ways than one. "Yes. I did."

"Did you find a boy?" mom asked with a knowing smirk.

"Maybe," I answered as I pulled the bags out of my trunk and walked into the house.

"Is he cute?" she asked.

"Duh," I said.

"How old is he?" Dad asked.

"Twenty," I said though I wasn't completely positive. Why hadn't I talked to him more? I had spent more time in lion form than human.

"How big is he?" Mom asked.

I set my bags down in my bedroom and turned around to face them. "Human form he is about six feet tall. Lion form he is almost as big as dad."

Dad and mom seemed shocked by that. "Really?" Dad asked. "You sure you weren't just confused because you are so small?"

I stuck my tongue out at him and said, "He was almost as big as Marcus and as I recall you said Marcus and you are the same size. Therefore, he is almost as big as you."

"That's impressive," Mom said. "Do not mess it up."

I snarled at her. "Thank you for your vote of confidence, Mom."

She smiled and patted my head. "You are welcome, dear. Now, get your homework done. You have school tomorrow."

Dad smiled and hugged me. "I'm glad you are safe. I take it you enjoyed your time with that pride?"

I nodded my head. "Yeah. I really liked it there."

Dad sighed and whispered, "It pains me to say it because you are the only cub I have right now, but if you want to join that pride, I will allow it."

It was an incredibly nice gesture and one I had not expected my dad to give me. "Thank you, Dad."

He ruffled my hair and said, "I just want the best for you Now, do as your mom said and get your homework done."

"Yes, alpha," I said in a monotone voice.

He laughed and shut my bedroom door. I flopped onto my back on my bed and called Iagan. He answered on the first ring. "You in one piece?"

I rolled my eyes. "No, I broke into six."

"You need me to come over and glue you back together?" he asked with a laugh.

"No."

He laughed again. "Okay, well you better get your homework done so you don't get grounded."

How did he know I had homework?

"Yes, sir," I said sarcastically.

"Text me later," he said and then hung up.

I stared at the phone a moment and then sighed happily. I had no idea if this was going to work out or not, but I was happy I had finally found a male. I had to stay positive and just hope it did. I closed my eyes and remembered the night of the attack. Was it fate? Was I meant to find him again since he had saved me?

I had to admit that it was a definite plus for him that he had already proven he could protect me. I felt incredibly embarrassed that I had not remembered him. Why had I suppressed that piece of my memory? I grabbed my backpack and pulled out my school books. As much as I hated homework, I knew it was a necessary evil in order to keep my straight A's. Plus, I had to read ahead for my college mythology class. Professor Cleo asked us to read a lot and write our thoughts about the reading during the week so I tried to do as much on the weekends as possible.

I was focused on my homework when I heard hissing and loud crashing down the hall. I sighed. Mom was most likely fighting again. I recalled the nice, calm environment at Sheila and Iagan's pride and wished I was there. Was dad serious about letting me join their pride? And how would that even work? Wouldn't Iagan and I have to create our own pride if we became mates?

"Dinner!" Dad yelled.

I sighed again. Maybe he would let me take my food to my room if I said I had homework still. I set my mythology book on my bed and headed towards the dining room. I walked in the room and was surprised to see Mom with a swollen eye. I looked away from her and looked at my dad instead. "Can I eat in my room? I am not done with my homework yet."

Dad studied my face a moment and then nodded. "Sure."

I grabbed my plate and filled it with food from the table and then headed to the kitchen to grab a soda before heading back to my room and turning on my TV. I sent Sheila a text, *"Ever wonder what life would be like if the supernaturals could come out and be visible to the humans?"*

She wrote back a moment later. *"All the time. I don't think the humans could handle seeing giant Smilodons walking around. Their instincts would tell them to flee in fear and they would go crazy."*

I laughed. Yeah, she was right about that. *"I think when I graduate I want to go visit the unicorns."*

"I've never seen a unicorn! You have to let me go with you!"

"Definitely!" It made me happy that I had finally found a female my age to talk to. I had had a friend when I was younger, but she had moved out of state to join another pride.

I talked with Sheila a bit longer while I finished my homework and then went to bed.

CHAPTER THREE

Iagan and I had been texting off and on since I had woken up at six a.m. I had behaved during mythology, though, not wanting to get in trouble with Professor Cleo. Plus, I actually wanted to pay attention in that class. She had assigned us a group project so I was sitting on a bench outside of the English building, talking with my group.

"I think we should do the Norse gods," one of the girls said.

I rolled my eyes. She had probably never heard of them until the comic book movie came out featuring two of the gods. "There will be at least three other groups doing them. We should be different and do the Egyptian deities."

"Why not the Greek?" one of the only guys in the class suggested.

I stood up and said, "As soon as you guys decide, just send me an email, and I'll get to work on it. I have to go to school though."

"Are you sure?" the guy asked.

I nodded and started walking backwards. "I don't care which ones we do our project on because I like all of them.

"Okay," they said and started discussing it again.

I shook my head at them, knowing they would not come to a

decision for a while and then backed into someone. I spun around, completely shocked that I had not smelled a person behind me since they were upwind of me. It was a very attractive guy, and I hid my surprise as best as I could. I had never seen this guy here at the college before and judging by the pack on his back, he was a wanderer.

"Hello," he said in a sultry growl that made every hair on my arms and legs stand on end. I took a deep breath and confirmed what I had thought. He was a werelion.

"Hi," I said with purr in my voice. "Can I help you?"

"I couldn't help but stop when I smelled you," he whispered. "Your scent is intoxicating."

"Are you a new student?" I asked. "I haven't seen you around here before." God he was sexy. His hair was black as the night and his eyes were a perfect shade of amber. He was muscular, tall, and dangerous looking. I bet he could take down every guy at this school without breaking a sweat or messing up his hair.

"No, but I could be if it would ensure that I would be around you often," he said as he walked closer, circling me as he assessed me.

He was a nice flirter, but I was not interested in being his second mate and I was positive he already had one. I looked at his clothes again and was shocked to realize they were actually very nice. His shoes looked brand new.

"Where are you from?" I asked him as I began circling him. I knew others probably thought we looked crazy, but I did not like him circling me while I stood still. It made me feel like prey, and I was *not* prey.

"I'm from down south, but I wanted a change of scenery for a vacation," he said and then stopped, standing in the grass out of the way of the students walking to and from class.

"How long will you be here?" I asked. By law he had to contact the local pride's alpha within four days to discuss why he was here.

"I've been here two days and have been searching for the local pride. It seems I found one," he said with a smile. "How old are you?"

"Seventeen, eighteen soon," I answered. "I can give you the alpha's phone number and address if you want?" Why wasn't he taking the hint?

"Are you his?" he asked as he stepped closer to me, inhaling loudly and then purring.

"I'm courting," I answered. Even though it was true, for some reason I felt like I should have simply said I was claimed. Why? I had not made a commitment to Iagan yet.

He smiled wide. "That makes my day much better. It means there is still hope. Can you take me to your alpha?"

I was supposed to treat others with respect and show them great kindness, but I had school and I knew Dad would forgive me for not showing him to the house. "I would, but I have to go to school."

"Can I take you?" he asked.

Most girls would have been frightened with a male so pushy at this point, but it only made me feel wanted. He was hot and definitely looked like he could handle himself in a fight. My phone vibrated with a text message, but I ignored it, not wanting to talk to Iagan while I was near this guy. I had a hunch that he would try to ruin my courting with Iagan if he could.

"You promise not to harm me?" I asked.

He became very serious and whispered, "I promise that no harm will come to you while you are in my presence."

That promise had a lot of other meanings to it. He had not only sworn not to harm me, but to protect me while I was with him. I would have just driven my car, but Dad had taken it to get the oil changed.

"I accept your offer of a ride to school."

He smiled and said, "Great. Please follow me."

I followed him to the parking lot and was incredibly pleased when he stopped next to a beautiful black motorcycle. I had always wanted to ride a motorcycle. "Your bike is gorgeous," I said as I put the helmet he had offered me on.

"Thank you," he said. "It took me a long time to save for it, but she was worth every penny."

"What's your name?" I asked him as he climbed onto the bike.

"Ethan."

He started his bike and I hopped on, holding on to him as best as I could with his pack on his back. The scent of lion on him was stronger than any I had smelled before. It called to my primitive side and made me want to change forms and go play in the woods with him. I gave him directions when we stopped at the first stoplight and then enjoyed the ride and the nearness of such a dominant male. I bet he and my dad were the same size.

He stopped in front of the school, and I climbed from his bike, taking the helmet off and hoping I didn't have helmet-hair.

"Thank you for the ride," I said as I handed him the helmet and tried to regain my composure.

He took the helmet and then used the kick stand to prop the bike up before walking to me and holding his cell phone out. "Would you please give me your alpha's number? I think I would like to stay in this area for a while."

I took it and typed in my dad's information. "Let him know that I referred you to him."

He took the phone and purposefully let his hand graze across mine. Electricity shot up my arm, and I had to resist the urge to purr. "Would you like to go to dinner with me?" he asked.

I almost responded with yes, but stopped myself. "I'm sorry, but I can't."

He stepped closer to me and whispered, "Tonight. Six o'clock. I'll speak to your alpha and then we will go."

I moved closer to him and whispered into his ear, "I already told you that I can't. I'm sorry, but I won't be an addition to your pride."

He laughed a deep rich laugh. "You think you will find a male who is dominant enough to keep you, but will only want one female?"

I shrugged. "One can only hope."

His eyes widened a little in shock, but he recovered quickly. "Wear something nice," he said. "We'll be going to a nice restaurant."

"I appreciate your interest, I really do, but I cannot accept your invitation," I said in a "no argument" tone.

He smiled. "We'll see how long you keep saying that, darling. By the way, what's your name?"

"Ainsley."

He leaned close, letting his cheek brush mine and whispered, "See you tonight, Ainsley." As he pulled away, he kissed my cheek and then climbed onto his bike.

I watched him walk away with butterflies in my stomach. Why was I even thinking about going on a date with him when I had a sexy guy like Iagan interested in me? I shook my head sadly. I knew exactly why, he had the bad boy charm. We all knew how that would end though, with me being sad and him finding some other dumb chick to fall for him.

"Who was that?" Felix asked with disdain in his voice.

"A friend," I answered, not wanting to talk to him about it. I pulled my cell phone out of my pocket and found a picture message from Iagan. He did have a nice body and was attractive. I saved the picture and asked him when we could go out. I needed to be near him, to forget Ethan.

"So, how was your weekend?" Felix asked as we walked together.

"Productive," I said with a smirk. "I finished all of my shopping."

"Hey," Theresa said as we merged together and headed towards class. "How was your weekend shopping?"

"I totally scored," I said with a smile. Theresa looked at me curiously, and I said, "On my shopping. Dirty mind."

She shook her head. "Whatever, chica."

"How were your weekends?" I asked.

They smiled sheepishly, and my shoulders relaxed in relief, knowing now that Felix would no longer try to date me because he and Theresa were interested in each other.

"We played a lot," she said.

"Fun," I said with a smile. My cell phone vibrated so I pulled it out of my pocket and checked the message from Iagan.

"I'll see you tomorrow."

"Tomorrow? Where?"

"It's a surprise."

"I hate surprises." Especially if it meant he might cross paths with Ethan. I did not want to see Iagan fight Ethan.

"You'll like this one."

We sat down at our desks in the classroom, and I put my phone away and then put my face in my hands. I knew I had to trust that Iagan could protect himself. If he couldn't, then I should not have him as a mate. Yet I wanted to keep him and Ethan apart if possible. I did not want Ethan, but I knew he wanted me and he would probably do almost anything to get me if he truly wanted me.

Once again, I was forced to explain how to solve the math problems to Theresa and Felix, but today they were too sidetracked by looking at each other and smirking that they still did not understand the math at the end of class. As we walked down the hallway towards the cafeteria, I saw Chuck looking at me as he stood in the middle of his group. I had forgotten all about the football game and him asking me to go to it in the first place.

"Hey, Ainsley," Chuck said with a smile.

I stopped, and Felix and Theresa continued on towards the cafeteria. Part of me felt hurt that they would abandon me so easily, but I knew it was a good thing. Maybe I would have to find some new friends if they really got serious about each other. I refused to be a third wheel.

"Sup Chuck?" I said with a smile back to him.

"What happened to you after the game? I saw you at the beginning, but when I looked for you afterwards, you were gone." Why did it bother me that he seemed upset? Was I imagining the whiney tone in his voice?

"Sorry, I had to go home. Family emergency," I lied easily. Humans were stupid and very easy to lie to.

"It's all good," he said, "But I was glad that you were up in the stands cheering for me."

I smirked. "Who said I was cheering for you? Maybe I was cheering for the other team…"

He laughed. "I highly doubt that." He flexed his bicep and said, "None can resist me."

I rolled my eyes at him. If only he knew how weak he really was. One arm wrestling match with me and he would forever feel like a wimp. "*Riiiight*," I said. "Well, I need to go get food. I'll talk to you later."

"I'll buy you lunch," he offered.

I almost snarled at him. I would *never* accept food from a human. "No, thank you," I said as politely as I could. "I make it a point never to accept food from anyone. Sorry."

I walked away from him before he made me angrier. I knew that he had no idea the customs of my clan, but I was still mad that he had offered to buy me food. Did I seem poor? Did he think I did not dress in nice enough clothes? I looked at myself in the reflection of the cafeteria's windows. I was five foot seven with long legs and curves that most girls wished they had. I thought my face was moderately attractive, but I had been told by others that I was beautiful and should be a model. I was seriously contemplating the career since I would not have to do anything except smile and pose.

My clothes looked like most other girls, slim fitting jeans

from the mall, and a t-shirt from one of the uppity stores that fit tight against my body. Was I just overthinking it? Was he just trying to be nice?

"Earth to Ainsley," Felix said. "Are you going to get lunch or just stare out the window at the nerds all day?"

I looked through the window and confirmed what he had said. I was staring at the nerds and they were cowering and looking very frightened of me. Oops. "Sorry, I was spacing out and looking at my reflection."

"Well, the line is super long already," Theresa said as she walked to us from the cafeteria. "You better hurry before it gets any longer and you miss out on lunch completely."

I hurried inside and joined the line of shuffling, gossiping students and pulled out my cell phone to text Sheila about the cattle that my school consisted of.

"Ainsley, that is such a cute shirt," Camille said from behind me.

"Thanks," I said, ignoring her and continuing my text of *"OMG the cheerleader sheep is talking to me now."*

"So, why haven't you signed up for any sports? We all know you are super athletic," she asked.

Was she baiting me into something? I had never signed up for sports and the only reason she knew I was athletic was because of me whipping her butt in every sport during PE. "I don't have any interest in sports here."

"Ah, so you don't like competition," she said. I looked up and saw the smirk on her face and wanted to smack it off of her.

I put my phone away and said, "Oh, I love competition, but the others get too upset when I beat them. It seems most everyone else can't handle the competition." The line moved forward, and I moved away from her, going to the opposite side of the long buffet-like table to pick out my food. I paid for the food and then headed out of the cafeteria, feeling Camille's eyes on the back of my head the entire time. Something was going on with that girl, and I did not like it. I would have to keep my distance from her. The rest of the day flew by, and I rushed home, wanting to burn off some of my pent-up energy, so glad that Dad had dropped my car in the school parking lot after lunchtime.

As I pulled into the driveway, my heart began to beat faster. There, next to my dad's pickup truck, was Ethan's motorcycle. I turned off my car and walked into the house cautiously.

"Ainsley," Dad called from his study.

I walked to it, taking a deep breath for courage and stepped inside with a smile on my face. "Yes, sir?"

Ethan turned and smiled at me. "Hello again."

Dad waved his hand at the chair opposite him, the only chair left aside from the one Ethan was sitting in. "Please sit down."

I did as he asked, feeling incredibly nervous. Ethan continued to smile at me, which made my nervousness even worse. Why was he smiling so happily? What had he done?

I looked at my dad and he said, "Ethan here has asked for permission to court you."

That sneaky jerk! I was going to get him for this. "Has he?" I asked calmly.

Ethan nodded, his face taking on a serious edge. "I am in need of a mate and so far you seem to be a promising female."

Promising? What did that mean? "What are my options?" I asked my dad.

Dad sighed. "I knew you were going to ask that. Ethan, would you please leave me to speak with her a moment?"

Ethan stood up. "Of course." He walked to the back of the room and said, "Please, take your time. I will wait outside until you are ready for me again."

Dad waited until he heard the front door shut before meeting my eyes. "You don't have very many options here, Ainsley."

"Why not?" I asked him. "If I don't like him, then I don't have to take him as a mate, right?"

Dad leaned back in his chair and said, "No. Unfortunately that is not how it works for you."

"How does it work?" I asked him nervously. I didn't like where this was heading. It wasn't really that I had no interest in courting Ethan, but I hated being told what to do and he seemed very bossy.

"If a male comes and asks to court you, then you must, as a free female, court him. If he proves not to be dominant enough, or there is some major provable flaw, then you can deny him being your mate. But if he is dominant enough, and there is nothing technically wrong with him, then you must accept him as a mate. In this circumstance, you'd have to have a *really* good reason not to accept him."

"Why didn't you tell me this before?" I asked him angrily. "I thought that as females, we had the most power over choosing mates because there were so few of us?"

"I didn't think we would have to deal with this with you," he said. "There hasn't been a male around here for ten years. I know you and the male from Marcus' group are courting, but by our laws, you must also allow Ethan to court you as well."

"Why? Why can't I just tell him that I'm choosing Iagan?" I asked angrily, standing up and putting my hands on his desk.

Dad met my eyes a moment and asked, "Can't you tell what Ethan is? Surely you are not that blinded by that other male that you can't sense what he is."

I sat down and shook my head. "I don't know what you are talking about. Ethan is very dominant, but that's all."

"Have you smelled him?" Dad asked.

I nodded. "He smells very much like a lion while in his man form. So?"

Dad sighed and leaned his head back, looking up at the ceiling. "I knew I should have tutored you more." He dropped his chin down and looked at me. "He is a Ra, the most powerful of all alphas, obtaining the name because he is a descendent of the God

Ra. There are only three known to exist. I don't know where he has been hiding, but a male like him is capable of taking over the entire country if he wanted to." He swallowed, and I realized that my father was nervous. "I cannot protect you from him, Ainsley. He is more powerful than me."

Fear like none I had ever felt before consumed me. My father was never frightened of anyone. He never admitted when another could defeat him and he never backed down. He was always willing to fight until his death if need be. For him to admit that he could not protect me was major and a definite sign that I needed to listen to him and take what he said about Ethan seriously.

"You don't know what you are either, do you? Your mother never told you?" he asked.

Of course she had told me, I just did not believe her. "She told me that I am a Sekhmet, but I never really understood what that meant." I said with a shrug of my shoulders.

"You are a Sekhmet because you are a descendent of Sekhmet. Sekhmet was a war lioness and a goddess. She was mainly worshipped by the Egyptians."

"Doesn't that mean that I am related to Ethan, so I can't mate with him because that would be incest?" I asked hopefully. I had heard Mom talk about Ra and Sekhmet before, but I had dismissed her talking as crazy stories. Why hadn't I listened to her?

"No, it means that you are ideal mates, because your child would be a descendent of both deities. Go get Ethan, let me talk with him and then grab snacks and come back here. I need to tell you everything about our background and prepare you for your future."

I was afraid, but I did as he asked, walking outside to where Ethan was leaning against a tree beside the house. At my approach he stood and walked towards me. "Is he ready to see me?" he asked.

I nodded. "Please return to his office."

His smile wilted and he looked at my face seriously. "What's wrong? You seem upset."

"It is nothing that you need to concern yourself with," I said as I turned and headed back towards the house. If he really cared, then he would just leave and let me live my life how I wanted. I would date Iagan and instead of traveling for a mate, we would travel the world for fun. It would be glorious and I would have babies and then we would grow old together with a small pride that truly loved each other. What would my life be like if I had to take Ethan as a mate?

Ethan did not say anything else as he walked into the house and to my father's study. I headed to the kitchen, preparing snacks of meats, cheeses and fruits and set it all on a tray so it was easier to carry once my father was done talking to Ethan. Why was this happening to me? Sure, most females would be thrilled that there were two males attempting to court them. Especially since both were very attractive and strong. How strong was Ethan? If my father was scared of him than he was definitely someone to be feared. Wait, if I was a descendent of Sekhmet, then that meant that my mom was, too. So why wasn't she stronger? Or was my dad a descendent? But then why wasn't he stronger?

"Hello, sweetheart. How are you?" Stacy asked as she walked to the fridge and pulled out a cold bottle of water.

"I've been better," I said and leaned on the kitchen counter on my elbows.

"What's wrong, Sugarplum?" she asked with a smile. "What does a pretty girl like you have to be upset about?"

Stacy was nice and even if my mom hated her for being one of my dad's other mates, I got along with her well. She always bought me the cutest clothes for Christmas and made sure that I never felt forgotten in our mostly adult pride.

"I'm having lion problems, but I can't really talk about them until after I talk with Dad," I said as I watched her make a sandwich.

She stopped and looked at me. "Well, whatever it is, I'm sure your dad can handle it and will help you as best as he can."

If only he could handle it for me. "Stacy, can I ask you a question?" I asked quietly so that my mother, who was using the computer in her bedroom wouldn't hear.

She walked over to me, leaning her hip against the counter and whispered, "Anything. You know that."

"Why hasn't my mom killed Lucy?" I whispered as quietly as I could.

Stacy heaved a big sigh. "Perhaps you should ask your mom that."

I looked at her like she was crazy. "Stacy, come on."

She laughed. "Alright. I'll tell you, but if your momma asks you, don't say it was me."

"Yes, ma'am."

She bit her lip a second and said, "It's really two things. One, I'm not sure which one of them would win if they got into a true to the death fight. Lucy may act ditsy and look frail, but that girl packs one hell of a punch. Two, it's really looked down upon for mates to kill each other. We are supposed to live to protect the pride and to please our mate. Obviously, killing his other mate would not please him and killing one of the lionesses could also hurt the pride if we were to be attacked and had one less body to help fight."

"Would Dad really be so upset if Mom killed Lucy?" I asked. I knew she was his favorite, but I figured that was just because she was his favorite in the bedroom.

Stacy shrugged. "I don't know for sure, but I know one time your mom tried to kill her and your dad got between them. Ever since then, their relationship has not been the same. I don't know if your mom resents your dad for stopping her or if your dad is holding a grudge for your mom almost killing Lucy."

I frowned. "Dad doesn't hold grudges."

Stacy tapped her finger to her nose. "Exactly."

"Isn't there some way for my mom to break the mating agreement with my dad? So that she could leave to find someone else?"

"Breaking your mating bond is a very serious and dangerous thing," Stacy said. "It's a combination of extreme pain and lots of magic." She shook her head. "Don't ask me how it works because I really don't understand all the magic involved. I just know that some people die instead of breaking the bond. Plus, I know she did not want to even consider it while you were a child. There is no way that your father would have let her take you away from him."

That answered those questions and added to the negativity I was already dealing with.

"Why aren't there more prides with females having multiple males? We outnumber the males." I asked.

"Prides have always been a patriarchal society. When the male population began to dwindle, we slowly began to see females with multiple males, but it was only the very strong females. And, most of us are tired enough dealing with one lion male, that we couldn't handle more. You'll understand when you're older."

So, the males were the problem. "Thanks, Stacy."

She hugged me one-armed and said, "Anytime. And whatever you're dealing with, just remember that you are part of a select few of the greatest lionesses ever. There's nothing you can't handle."

What did she mean by that? I didn't get the chance to ask though, because Dad walked into the kitchen and crooked his finger at me. "Time to talk," he said.

I grabbed the tray of food, and Dad grabbed a couple of bottles of water from the fridge and we headed to his study. Judging by the mad lock on his face, this conversation was not going to be fun for either of us. I set the tray down on his desk and then scooted one of the chairs closer so that I would not have to lean very far to grab food while we talked. I would have eaten some of what was already there, but it was proper protocol for the alpha to eat first. Not that dad would have reprimanded me, but I was trying to behave for once.

He sat down in his chair and for once he looked his age. He had black hair with some light grey peppering that had come in only this year, high cheekbones, and a strong jaw. He looked like he could kill you and not even think twice about it, and that was mostly true. I had seen him kill men and I had seen him save them. He was the alpha, the leader of our pride, and the most level-headed person I knew. This was the first time I had ever seen him truly scared and acting like he had no idea what to do.

"So," I said to break the silence and pull him from his thoughts. "What does it mean that I'm Sekhmet?"

"Sekhmet was a goddess," he began, "who was sent down to frighten humans and get them to pray. She took the form of a lion and came down here, eating humans and drinking their blood. The plan worked, she made the humans pray to the gods again, but the problem was that she liked eating the humans too much. She did not want to return to the sky and her previous diet. The gods did not want to attack her because they loved her and knew she was consumed by bloodlust, a fate that any one of them would share if they had killed as many as she had. So, after much deliberation, Ra decided that he would come down and talk to Sekhmet. He came down in his regular form, but she had stayed as a lion too long and could not remember how to return to her other form. Ra took pity on his fellow god and also felt a connection to her. So, he took on the form of a lion and mated with her."

"She let him?" I asked in shock. "Just like that?"

Dad laughed and shook his head. "No, they had a great fight and it was only after Sekhmet decided that he was the best possible mate for her that she decided to mate with him. So, they mated and when she became pregnant, the bloodlust left and she was able to return to her regular form, for the most part."

"What does that mean?" I asked. "Did she stay in her battle form?" We could take three forms like the storybooks said, human, lion and halfway between the two. We called it battle form because we only used it when battling.

"Whenever she took her regular form, she still had the head of a lion, which is why the ancients always depict her with the head of a lion."

That made sense except a lot of the other gods had animal heads, too. Before I could ask he said, "The others were depicted with animal heads because some humans had witnessed them changing shape. It was more efficient to draw them with the animal heads than to draw two separate pictures of them."

"What does this mean for me? How does this pertain to us?" I asked. I really wanted him to get to the point.

He ate a piece of cheese and then motioned at the tray for me to eat as well. I gladly took some meat and cheese and ate them in one giant bite. "You are descended from Sekhmet's mating with other gods, and their offspring mating with others until us. It means you are stronger and faster than others, more dominant than most, and there are only a handful of you still alive anymore. Or at least, that we know of. There could be a group of you living underground for all I know, but for the sake of the discussion we will just say that you are one of the last alive."

"So Ethan is from Ra and because of that he is stronger and faster and more dominant as well?" I asked. "Stronger than a regular alpha?"

Dad nodded. "Exactly. Which is why you and Ethan would be an ideal couple, because there are only a few of you left and your offspring would be stronger than any others."

That was hard to believe. "But why does that mean I must choose him?" I asked. "Why can't I choose who I want?"

"He would destroy any other male you hoped to mate with.

Also, your bloodlines could rejuvenate the entire werelion clan and bring us into a greater and higher place among the paranormals. It could even mean the possibility of the paranormals taking the world back over," he said in an awed whisper.

I rolled my eyes. "You and I both know that will never happen. There are too many humans with too much technology and fire power. They would blow us to bits before we could kill them all." Tanks were very thick and made of very hard metal. Even our claws had trouble getting into them.

"I rarely make you do things you do not want, Ainsley, but you must do this. You must let him court you and possibly take you as his mate. He does not seem like he is that bad of a guy. You might actually like him."

I doubted it.

"What happens if I refuse?" I asked him.

Dad's face grew very grim and he said, "Then he will challenge me for the pride and I will be forced to fight him. Please, Ainsley, do not make me do that."

A fearful alpha was a disturbing thing. "Alright," I whispered. "I will let him court me, but I would like to state for the record that I do not like it and I will try to find some way to get out of it."

Dad smiled. "I expect no less from you." He took another bite of food, letting his calm demeanor take over. "Would you like to go on a run with me?"

I nodded without hesitation. It had been months since we had gone on a run together. "I have one more question," I said quickly.

"Ask," he said.

"If I am a descendent of Sekhmet, then that means that mom or you is a descendent, right? So which one of you is it?"

"Neither," he said and then his gaze softened. "You know I love you?"

I nodded, but did not like where this was going.

"It is something your mother does not like to talk about so I'm sure that is why she has not told you. Plus, it is something I suppose I should have told you myself."

Oh, no.

"When I met your mother, she was living in a small house in the middle of the suburbs. She was docile and could pass very easily for human. I was twenty at the time and I liked your mother. So, I stayed at the hotel a few miles from her house and watched her and her mate at the time. Her mate was old, and I knew I could defeat him. I was young, stupid and cocky." He took a deep breath and continued. "I waited until her mate had left and then I knocked on her door. She welcomed me in, being kind and accommodating to a fellow werelion. I exclaimed my desire for her and told her that I was going to take her away from the humanity she was being forced into. She tried to tell me she was happy, but I could see a sort of deadness in her eyes. So, that night when her mate came back, I challenged him. We drove to the middle of nowhere and battled. I had underestimated the old man. He was Sekhmet and even in his old age he was very strong. It was a two day battle that I barely won and once we had finished, I claimed your mother and brought her back here. Unbeknownst to me and her, was that she was already pregnant with you."

"So, I'm not yours?" I asked softly.

"You are mine and will always be my daughter. I helped your mother give birth to you and I have raised you. As far as I am concerned, you could have very easily been mine if I had challenged him only a few days earlier."

I sat very still, letting it all sink in. I felt no different towards my father because he had raised me and it did not matter to me who had contributed. Yet part of me felt betrayed at not being told this before.

"Well, that explains a few things," I whispered.

"You are mine, Ainsley. I even chose your name."

I smiled at him. "I know, Dad. I'm just absorbing it all. I've learned quite a bit today."

He smiled. "Yes, you have. I am proud of you for taking it all in stride though."

"So, is that why mom is so unhappy here? Because she had been the only mate and now she isn't?" It would make sense to me. Especially if she actually loved my biological father.

Dad nodded. "Yes."

Someone knocked on the door and then my mom stuck her head inside. "Are you busy, Aldric?" she asked my dad.

My dad shook his head. "No, we just finished. How can I help you?"

She looked at me and asked, "Can we speak in private?"

I sighed and grabbed my bottle of water and a handful of food from the plate. "I'll go change and wait in the forest."

Mom grabbed my wrist as I walked by and stared into my eyes with a weird passion that I had never seen on her face before. "I love you, Ainsley. I want you to remember that."

Mom was not a very affectionate woman. We never hugged or said I love you, and I was okay with that. This was not like her.

"I know, Mom," I said honestly. "I love you, too."

Tears formed in the corners of her eyes, and she released me. "Good. Thank you."

I walked out of the room feeling very nervous about my mother. She was never emotional in front of me, never crying or anything. The only emotion I ever saw from her was anger when she and Lucy got into it. What was going on?

I walked out of the house and headed to the forest. I had a feeling Dad and Mom would be talking for a while so I sat down and ate the food in my hand and enjoyed the cool breeze that blew the various scents of my home to me. I could smell the pine trees all around me, squirrels that lived in the trees, each lion in my pride and the lingering scents from Ethan.

I did not want to think about him so I took out my cell phone and sent Iagan a message. *"What time will you be seeing me and where? There's something we need to talk about."*

I waited for his reply, but after five minutes I received nothing. Dad came out to me with a smile on his face and anger evident in his posture. "Ready?"

I nodded. "I was born ready. You think you can beat me this time, old man?"

He rolled his head around, stretching his neck out. "I feel good about today. I think it might be the day I regain my pride."

"It's only been six years since the last time you beat me," I said sarcastically.

He growled at me and stripped his shirt off. "Keep talking, little girl."

I hid behind a tree as I changed. Not that I wasn't used to changing, but now that I was older I did not like the idea of my father seeing me naked. Once we were changed, we walked over to a tree with a red flag tied to it and squatted down, swishing our short tails back and forth as we prepared to start.

I knew I was still a child in werelion standards, but normally I did not notice it. Standing next to my dad's giant size, I was definitely aware that I was a child. He growled once and we tightened our muscles. He growled again and I focused on the open stretch of forest in front of me. I was not going to let him win. He roared, and we leapt forward, running as fast as we could down the path. I barely let my paws touch the ground before I lifted them again. My stride was as long as I could make it, stretching my body out as far as it would go. We were ambush animals, so long races were not our best, which is what made it the most fun. Dad stayed nose to nose with me for the first twenty yards and then I pulled ahead of him, passing by the tree with the other red flag a full neck ahead.

I roared victoriously and said, *"I won. I won. I won."* Telepathically to him.

He leapt at me, swatting his giant paw at my shoulder, but I darted out of the way just in time. *"Come back here and let me cut you down to size."*

I rolled my eyes at him and swiped at him as he came towards me again. *"Totally cliché saying."*

He hissed at me, and I ran around a tree, making him claw the tree instead of me. *"Missed me."*

"Come here and I'll show you cliché."

We ran around for a couple hours and then Lucy and Stacy came out to play. I left them to play together and grabbed my clothes between my teeth as I headed towards the house. I pushed down on the front door handle and pushed the door open with my head. I walked to my room and changed forms and clothes, putting my pajamas on. I grabbed my cell phone and unlocked it and was pleased to finally find a text message from Iagan.

"I'll see you tomorrow for dinner. Are you breaking up with me? Already? LOL."

I sighed, not sure what to say to that except, *"I can't wait to see you. And no."*

I needed to eat dinner and then I needed to go to sleep. Changing and playing with dad had made me incredibly tired. After making my dinner and watching some stupid reality television, I went to sleep, praying to any god that existed, including Ra and Sekhmet, that I could figure out what to do about Ethan and Iagan.

CHAPTER FOUR

"There's no way you could bench press as much as me. You are much smaller than me," Theresa argued as we walked towards the cafeteria.

If only she knew that I could throw a car without breaking a sweat. "Whatever makes you feel better, Theresa. But I am telling you that I can definitely bench, squat and anything else better than you."

We grabbed our food and returned to our normal spot. "Fine, let's test this out. I challenge you to an arm wrestling match," Theresa said seriously.

Part of me knew it was probably not a great idea to arm wrestle her, but another part of me felt like she was challenging my authority as the alpha of this pack. I knew it was not a real pack, but it was, in a way, a pack, and I was the leader, whether she wanted to believe that or not. Now I would prove it and put this to rest once and for all.

"Fine," I said around the bite of food in my mouth. "We'll have to find a table to do it on though." Not that I could not win on the ground, but it would give her less room to say the match was not legitimate.

She looked over to where Chuck's group was sitting at an outdoor table and said, "Why don't you ask your friend over there to let us use his table for a second."

I stood up and smiled. "Alright, let's go." We headed over and all of the jocks watched us suspiciously. I smiled at Chuck and asked, "Can we use your table for an arm wrestling match? It'll only take a second?"

He smiled at me and stood up, relinquishing his spot to me. "Sure thing." Since Chuck was the alpha of that group, the rest followed his lead and stood up. I sat down and Theresa sat across from me. The guys started taking bets, most betting on Theresa to win.

Oh, you poor, unknowing humans. I set my elbow on the table with my arm up and wiggled the fingers on my hand. "Ready?"

She gripped my hand with hers and smiled. "Ready to win."

Chuck put his hand on top of our joined ones and said, "Ready? Go!"

As soon as his hand released ours Theresa pushed against mine with all her might. I kept my arm immobile, simply holding her where she was and toying with her. She strained, and I was saddened at how weak she really was. I met her eyes and said, "Remember that you challenged me." I slammed the back of her hand down against the table, hard enough to hurt, but not hard enough to break anything. I wasn't trying to insult her or hurt her pride, but I wanted to make a point.

She turned and set her other hand on the table. "Again."

I sighed and this time slammed her hand down right away, not even giving her a chance to push against me.

Theresa stood up and rubbed her hands. "Damn."

One of the jocks took Theresa's place and put his arm on the table. "Let's go."

I had hidden my strength by avoiding everyone, but now I

wanted to show off a little. I gripped his hand and said, "Don't cry when you lose, okay?"

He rolled his eyes. "Okay, cupcake. Don't count your chickens before they hatch."

Chuck gripped our hands, and I tightened all of my muscles. I would make this match quick and would leave a bruise. This guy was cocky, and I did not like the sneer on his face.

As soon as Chuck said go, I slammed the guy's hand against the table. The crowd which had gathered around us made a collective "oh" which pleased me.

The guy switched arms, and I rolled my eyes. "After that you really think your other arm will be any better?"

"Go," he said with clenched teeth.

I sighed and gripped his hand. I'd let him struggle this time. Chuck released us, and I kept my elbow planted against the table, and my arm firmly at a ninety-degree angle. The guy strained until his face was red and a vein began to protrude on his forehead. He looked at me and I said, "What's wrong, cupcake?"

He growled and strained harder, but there was no use. I slammed his hand down and he walked away to nurse his wounded pride. I was about to stand up when someone else sat down in front of me. I looked up and found Ethan across from me.

"What are you doing here?" I asked angrily.

He set his arm on the table and smiled. "I don't think you're so tough," he said with a smile. "Come on. One match."

I met his eyes and said, "Why don't we place a wager on this match?"

"What kind of wager?" he asked.

"I win and you leave me alone, forever," I said as I continued to meet his gaze. Dad was right, he was *very* dominant.

"What if I win?" he asked, leaning over the table towards me. His scent wafted across the table and filled my nose. He smelled like home, not my physical home, but a home I had never known until then.

"If you win I will agree to let you court me," I said softly so that the humans would not hear. I did not need them spreading rumors about me.

He laughed. "You already have to do that," he said.

He was right, but... "If you win I will do it willingly," I said. It was the only thing I could think of to try to get rid of him. I already knew that I had to let him court me because I could not let him endanger my pride.

He stared at me in silence a moment and then wiggled his fingers. "Deal." I gripped his hand and a shiver ran through me. He smiled and asked, "You sure that you are ready?"

Chuck put his hand on top of ours and Ethan's eyes glowed amber. I inhaled deeply, calling upon my inner lioness for strength. Chuck released our hands and I pushed as hard as I could, using my arm and shoulder strength.

I did not expect to win right away, but as I pushed, I realized that I was very much outmatched.

Ethan held me in place and smiled. "You're very strong for a girl," he said. "But that is one of the reasons I want you." He pushed against me and no matter how hard I tried, I could not stop the slow descent of my hand.

"What's going on here?" Mr. Peterson, our principle asked.

My hand was only three inches away from the table now. I strained harder, trying to save myself somehow.

"Ainsley, who is this man?" he asked me.

"I don't know," I said through gritted teeth. "He sat down after I beat one of the other guys. I thought he was a new kid."

Ethan strained, pushing my hand down another quarter of an inch.

"Sir, I must ask you to leave," Mr. Peterson said. "This is a school and unless you have signed in at the front office to obtain a visitors pass then you are not welcome here."

"Almost done," Ethan said.

I held my arm where it was, not letting him gain any more ground. I could not lose. I could not let him win.

Mr. Peterson set his hand on Ethan's shoulder and said, "Now."

Ethan released my hand, spun around, and grabbed Mr. Peterson's hand off of his shoulder. "Do not touch me, sir."

I stood up and rubbed my shoulder, knowing I was going to be sore for at least an hour or two after that. I had not lost though, so I did not have to court him yet. "Come on, Theresa," I said softly. "Let's go to class."

Ethan walked towards the exit, but met my gaze for a second with a smirk on his face before I stepped inside the classroom. I knew I would see him again, but I was betting it would not be tonight.

Class passed by quickly, and I hurried home, hoping to have time to shower and change before I saw Iagan. As I pulled into the driveway, my hopes died at the sight of a strange Chevrolet Camaro parked in front of the house. It had to be Iagan. The car was beautiful, dark red with racing stripes down the center of it. I parked behind it and walked into the house. As soon as I stepped inside, I took a giant breath and smelled Iagan. He was here! A smile split my face and I followed his scent to my father's study, but the door was shut. I knocked lightly three times, but received no response. Dad knew I was there so why wasn't he letting me in? I hoped he wasn't telling Iagan about Ethan. I wanted to do that myself.

I headed to my room, grabbed a change of clothes, and then showered faster than ever before. I worked on my hair to ensure it was flowing and beautiful and then ran back to my room to put my other clothes away. I still did not receive a call from dad so I went to the kitchen and ate an apple while I waited nervously. What could they be talking about for so long?

I made a sandwich, hoping that eating would calm my nerves,

or at least make me less shaky. Five minutes later I was sitting on a barstool, tapping my foot and frustrated.

"Ainsley," Dad called softly. "Come here."

I hopped down from the barstool and walked as fast as I could without running. I opened the door and smiled at Iagan who was turned around and smiling at me. "Hey," he said pleasantly.

I sat down in the chair beside him. "Hello." He looked great in a tight fitting t-shirt and blue jeans. His smile was warm and inviting and made me wonder how soft his lips were. They looked incredibly soft.

I looked at my dad, pulling myself away from thoughts about how attractive Iagan was. "What's up?"

"Iagan here has expressed his interest in courting you. I expect you to be home by midnight. He will be staying the night tonight."

"Understood," I said quickly.

Dad sighed softly. "Then I suggest you leave now and go get her something to eat. She is very fidgety."

I stood up and hurried to the door, trying to urge Iagan out with my quickness. The last thing I needed was for Ethan to show up and ruin this.

"Thank you, sir," Iagan said before heading out of the study with me. We walked outside the house, and I climbed into his car before he could say anything to me.

He looked at my curiously, but started the car and drove down the driveway. "How are you today?" he asked.

"I'm great now that you're here," I said honestly.

He smiled and said, "I'm glad I am here, too."

"So, where are we going?" I asked. We needed to get away from the property and hopefully away from Ethan.

"I was thinking we could order some barbecue to go and then we could go play in your forest together," he said with a smile.

It sounded great, except it would end in catastrophe if Ethan showed up. "I like the first part, but why don't we go to a movie or something else afterwards instead? I'm not really in the mood to run around my forest."

He looked at me out of the corner of his eye, and I knew he could tell something was up. "You said you wanted to talk to me about something, right?"

Damn. "Yeah, but it can wait until later. It's really not that important."

He did not seem convinced, but he let it drop. "So, how was school?"

"Torturous," I said sarcastically.

He laughed. "You'll be done soon enough."

"Yeah, but then I will be going right back to college. I like college though."

"How do you know if you like college?" he asked.

We had barely talked about ourselves, but I had told him this. It hit home that I hardly knew him. And it made me wonder why I was so set on courting him instead of Ethan? Was it just because Ethan was so cocky? It was a turn off, but I did not know Iagan either. "I am taking a college class right now. I go two days a week during school hours," I explained. It made me a little mad that he didn't remember me telling them that at his pride's place.

"I think we should play a game," he said as he pulled into the right lane to turn into the Rib Shack.

"What kind of game?" I asked nervously.

"I ask you a question, you answer, and then you ask me a question and I answer. I want to get to know you better," he said.

He parked the car in an open spot and climbed out, rushing around to open my door for me. I stepped out and purposefully moved very close to him. "Thank you."

He smiled and inhaled my scent, purring a moment and whispered, "Anytime."

I stepped back, letting him take the lead and assume the dominant male role. "I'll go first then. When's your birthday?"

"November 29th. You?"

"June 25th."

"My turn," he said as he opened the door.

I stepped inside and stopped as a familiar scent blew into my nose. "Do you smell that?" I asked him softly.

He sniffed and shrugged. "Food, beer and humans."

How could he not smell the stench of werewolf? It was more prevalent to my nose than the humans. "Okay, your turn."

He asked for a table for two and then turned around. "Favorite color?"

"Green. What's yours?" I asked.

A human in his late thirties motioned for us to follow him so we obeyed, walking behind him as we headed towards our table. "Blue," Iagan said.

We sat down and I stacked my menu on top of Iagan's since we were getting ribs. "What's your favorite type of music?" I asked him.

He shrugged. "I like most anything. I have preferences in each genre, but I like them all."

He did not ask me what mine was so I waited as he thought. "What's your favorite time of year?"

"Winter," I said with a smile. "I love playing in the snow."

"Really?" he asked, shocked. "I would have taken you for a summer lioness."

I shook my head. "It's too hot and my fur is too thick for the summer."

"I love winter, too, but Spring is my favorite. It's not too hot and not too cool, plus there are lots of babies everywhere to eat."

There was a lot to eat in the spring, but winter was still my favorite. That did not count as my question since he willfully gave me the answer. "What is your favorite movie?" I asked him.

Our waitress came up and introduced herself. She was gorgeous with dark blue eyes, thick golden hair and a perfect physique. I looked at Iagan and was shocked to see him openly checking her out. Was he a human dater? I did not like the idea of my possible mate being into humans. It grossed me out.

"What can I get you two?" she asked cheerfully.

"We'll have two racks of rib and two iced teas," Iagan ordered with a flirtatious smile.

"I'll be right back with the drinks," the waitress said.

I waited until she was gone and gave Iagan my angry face. "Seriously?"

He stopped watching her walk away and looked at me. "What?"

"One, you're checking her out right in front of me. Two, she's *human*."

He at least had the decency to look a little embarrassed. "I'm sorry I did that. But what does it matter if she is human?"

Oh, my god. He was a human dater! I sat there in silent horror as I contemplated what I could say to him. He started laughing and it pulled me from my inner argument. "What?" I asked. "Why are you laughing?"

He smiled. "I was just testing you. Of course I would *never* date a human. What kind of freak do you take me for?"

I exhaled in relief and then scowled at him. "That was not nice. I was seriously freaking out."

"I know," he said, seemingly pleased with himself. "I could see the disgust on your face."

The waitress brought our drinks back and then left quickly. "I believe my question is still waiting to be answered by you," I said as I tried to recover still.

"What was it again? Favorite movie, right?" he asked. I nodded my head. "Well my favorite movie would have to be *Top Gun*."

Totally cliché guy movie. "What's your second favorite? *Die Hard*?" I asked him with a sarcastic smile.

He smiled at me and nodded. "Yep." I laughed, pleased that he at least had a sense of humor. "What's your favorite movie? Wait, let me guess...*Sex in the City*? Or *Twilight*?"

I rolled my eyes. "No way. *Tank Girl* is my favorite actually."

"Never heard of it," he said.

Figures. "It's a B movie. A cult classic."

"I'll have to look it up," he said.

"I can't believe you suggested *Twilight*," I said somewhat offended.

He shrugged. "Most girls your age are into that stuff."

"I'm not most girls," I said.

"I can see that," he said in a deep voice with a slight purr.

"What's your favorite food?" I asked and then took a drink from my iced tea in an attempt to calm myself.

"Water Buffalo."

I asked, "Where did you have water buffalo?"

"In Africa. I went on a long vacation around the world and met up with a werelion pride in Africa who took me on a hunt. It was a lot of fun."

It sounded amazing. I hoped I could go on an around the world vacation once I turned eighteen and graduated. "Were they nice?" I asked.

He nodded. "Yes. They were very accommodating. Now, to my next question since you just had three. What is the subject of the matter you need to discuss with me?"

I had hoped he would forget about it while we were playing this game.

"The subject is me," I answered with a smile.

"You're a smart aleck. Nice. What about you does it concern?"

"Us," I said letting my smile turn into a smirk.

He groaned. "Why don't you want to talk about it right now?"

"I would like to wait until after we have eaten," I said honestly.

The waitress brought our food out and he said, "Alright, but can we talk about it after we leave the restaurant?"

"You already asked three questions. The next one is mine."

He rolled his eyes at me and bit into his first rib. "You're going to be difficult. I can see that already."

"What female isn't difficult?" I asked with a laugh.

"None," he said. "And that is your question."

"That does not count!" I said around the rib meat in my mouth.

He smiled at me with sauce covering his mouth which made me laugh. We ate in silence after that, only talking again once we were heading outside. "What do you plan to do after you graduate?"

"It depends," I said honestly. "If I am single, then I will travel the world looking for a mate. If I have a mate, then I will have to discuss with him if we can travel for a little bit. If not, then I will just start college."

"Why are you so focused on finding a mate?" he asked.

"I don't know if you have noticed or not, but there are not that many males for me to choose from around here." There were even fewer single males.

He opened the door for me, and I climbed inside, putting my seat belt on and waiting for him to get in, knowing he was going to ask about the topic I was avoiding. He climbed in and drove to my house, parked the car and then turned and looked at me. "So, to the topic you texted me about and have been avoiding."

I sighed. Here it goes. "When I met you this weekend, you and your pride member were the first males my age I had seen in years. I was excited and then when I found out that you were the male who had saved me from that wolf it made my day even better."

"But?" he asked.

"The following Monday, yesterday, when I was at college, a werelion approached me. I had never seen him before and he had a big pack on his back that led me to believe he was a wanderer. He told me that he had stopped because he could smell me. I told him that I was already courting a male, but he said he was going to stick around and he met with my alpha. My alpha talked to me and apparently I cannot simply refuse or deny this male the chance to court me."

Iagan's body was very still, so still I could not tell if he was even breathing.

"I told my alpha I did not want to court this other male, but he told me that if I refused, the male would most likely challenge him and that would put my pride's lives on my conscience. I wish this was not happening, but there isn't much I can do. I really do not have a choice in the matter," I said. My voice had gone from a normal level to a whisper at the end. I waited for Iagan to say something, anything, but he simply sat still, staring out the front windshield.

What was he thinking? Was he mad at me? I hoped he knew that this was out of my control. If only I had been able to beat Ethan at arm wrestling!

"Are you interested in this other male?" he asked as he looked away from me, hiding his face, and I could tell, trying to hide his anger.

I didn't want to answer that. "Like I said, I have to court him because I don't want him to hurt my family."

"I will challenge him then," Iagan said. "After I beat him there will not—"

"No!" I said, interrupting him. "He's different than most alphas. He is—"

"You think I will lose?" Iagan asked. "You think I won't be able to beat him."

"You don't understand," I tried, but he interrupted me again.

"I will just have to prove myself to you." He opened his door and got out, walking to my door and opening it for me.

How could I fix this? I could not let him challenge Ethan. I couldn't let him throw his life away over me.

"Please listen to me," I begged him. He walked up to my house and opened the front door. "I know you are a strong alpha. I know you already protected me once, but—"

"And I will do it a hundred or a thousand more times if necessary," he said with steel in his voice. He leaned close to me and kissed me lightly on the lips. "Goodnight, Ainsley. I will see you tomorrow after you return from school."

"Iagan, I—"

He did not let me finish though. He pushed me gently inside and shut the door in my face. I stared at it and felt like I was useless. Had I just screwed myself out of a good guy? Was he going to get killed because of my stupidity?

"Ainsley?" Dad asked. "What's wrong?"

I groaned. "I may have made things incredibly worse," I whispered. "I tried to talk to Iagan about Ethan, but he wouldn't listen. He thought I was telling him that he was not strong enough to protect me. He refused to listen to me. I don't know what to do."

Dad hugged me against him and said, "I will talk to him tomorrow and explain things in detail to him."

"What if he won't listen?" I asked. "He wouldn't listen to me."

Dad laughed and pushed me back so I could see his face. "He *will* listen to me."

"I hope so," I whispered. "I do not want to see him killed over me."

"Go to bed and stop worrying. I will talk to him while you are at school."

"Thanks, Dad," I said, hugged him and then walked to my room. I hoped he could talk some sense into him. The last thing I needed was for him to challenge Ethan.

I closed my bedroom door and was about to change into my pajamas when I felt someone looking at me. I spun around in my room, but no one was there. I looked out my window, but the lights were on and it was dark outside so I could not see anyone. I shut my light off and returned to my window, but even my enhanced eyes saw nothing, but forest. Was I being paranoid? Had it been Iagan?

I shook my head and stepped away from the window. I really needed to calm down. I knew no one could get onto the grounds without my dad knowing. Maybe I had watched one too many horror movies.

CHAPTER FIVE

SCHOOL DRAGGED BY SLOWER THAN A NORMAL WEDNESDAY usually did. I tried to focus, but I could only think about Iagan. He had not been at the house before I had left for school, despite the fact that his car was still parked out front. I had tried to find Dad, but he wasn't anywhere to be found either. I hoped he was talking some sense into him and explaining how all of this was out of my control.

I drove home with nervous energy streaming through me. I planned to change as soon as I parked and to search out and kill anything that I could find. It had been hard not to hunt down one of the cheerleaders after listening to their high-pitched laughs. I parked at the house and was shocked to find Ethan's motorcycle, but not Iagan's Camaro parked there. Had they already fought? Or had Iagan seen him and just left? I rushed inside, straight to my dad's study and opened the door without knocking.

Dad and Ethan looked at me and Dad seemed genuinely surprised that I had barged in. "Can I help you?" Dad asked, glancing at Ethan nervously.

He didn't need to worry because Ethan was smiling at me and checking me out in my hip hugger jeans and low cut shirt. I resisted the urge to say something rude to him and asked Dad, "Did you take care of the thing you promised to?"

Dad nodded. "Yes. I'm sure the cat will return later, but for now it is off licking its wounds. I will talk with you about it more later," he said with a pointed look in Ethan's direction.

"Okay, thank you."

"Hello, Ainsley," Ethan said in a sexy voice.

My emotions were all over the place. Part of me was happy someone as dominant and attractive as Ethan wanted me, and part of me was mad that he was basically forcing me to court him. I wanted to snarl at him, but somehow my mouth smiled instead. "Hello, Ethan." I shook my head to try to clear it from this ridiculous feeling of happiness at his attention and said, "I'm going on a hunt. Call me if you need me." I dropped my phone in the front closet and then ran from the house before anyone could call me back or say anything. I changed forms as I ran, letting my clothes get ruined by being stretched out and torn into tiny little pieces. Mom hated when I did it, but now was not the day for me to waste time stripping out of them. I ran through the forest as fast as I could, burning off the anger and worry that I still felt.

I ran, hunted, killed, and ate for two hours straight. I finally calmed myself down enough to lay down on a tree branch and take a cat nap. I was almost asleep when I smelled Iagan approaching me.

I lifted my head and watched him walk towards me in his man form. "You really like sleeping in trees, huh?"

I yawned, ignoring his question. *"Are you ready to talk?"* I asked telepathically.

He sighed and sat down on the ground, leaning his back against a tree to face me. "I'm sorry I ignored you and jumped to conclusions. I misinterpreted what you were trying to tell me."

"Obviously. So, did my alpha explain it all to you?"

He nodded. "Yes."

"Ainsley?" Ethan called. "Are you out here?"

He knew I was out here. He could smell me. I leapt down from the tree and Iagan stood up, moving closer to me.

Ethan spotted me and smiled. "There you are. So, I was thinking I could take you to dinner tomorrow at—" He stopped talking when he finally caught Iagan's scent and saw him next to me. "Who are you?" he asked angrily, walking faster as he approached us.

"I'm Iagan, the one who is courting Ainsley," he said calmly. I had to hand it to him, he was acting calm despite knowing what Ethan was and having to feel how dominant he was.

Ethan looked Iagan over and then smirked. "Cute. Ainsley, can we talk?"

"No, because you can't hear me right now," I said sarcastically. Iagan smiled, having heard me, but his smile quickly disappeared when Ethan spoke.

"Actually, I can hear you. All of us *special beings* have telepathic links the moment we are born," he said smugly. He looked at Iagan and asked, "But why can you hear her?" He looked at me and spoke in a scolding tone, "You should not have given him a bond like that so early in your courtship."

"She gave it to me years ago," Iagan said. "When I rescued her."

"You rescued *her*? I highly doubt that," Ethan said.

"He did," I said, not wanting to go into any further detail.

"That does not matter," Ethan said. "Soon you will realize that this cub is not a match for you. You would be no better with him than you would be with a human."

Iagan growled. "Watch what you say to me. I will not stand by and be insulted."

Ethan smiled. "Would you like to challenge me? Please. It would make it easier on me than waiting for Ainsley to figure out that you are not the right one for her."

Before I could react, Iagan punched Ethan in the face. I knew the rules, and I knew that I was supposed to stay out of it once two males began fighting, but I did not want to see either one get hurt.

Wait, what? Either?

Ethan hit Iagan and the fight went into full swing. I wanted to call for my dad, but he could not interfere with their fight either. This was the way of our kind and only when one was forced to submit or knocked unconscious would the fight end. Or, if one of them died.

Ethan and Iagan fought with intense concentration, but both remained in human form. I watched them nervously, hoping that they would postpone the fight until later or indefinitely if it were up to me. The fight seemed to be evenly matched with neither really hitting the other more or landing more significant blows than the other. I watched Ethan and realized he wasn't trying his hardest. He had to be testing Iagan's strengths and weaknesses to fully assess his capabilities. It proved that he had been in many fights, and it was a sign of a better alpha and a better mate, whether I wanted to admit it or not. Iagan had not had the opportunity to learn such techniques yet because he had been under his alpha's thumb.

Ethan jumped back from Iagan and smiled. "You're a decent fighter, I'll give you that. However, you are no match for me."

Iagan growled. "Bring it."

Ethan's body began to twitch, and I knew what he was doing. He was shifting forms. Iagan put his hands behind his back and transformed them into paws with his claws extended. Ethan had no clue what he was jumping into. I could not let them get hurt. I leapt forward, changing in midair as I flew. Ethan leapt at Iagan in his battle form, claws stretched out and ready to slice him open, while Iagan stood still, waiting for his chance to use his claws against Ethan. I landed in front of Iagan as Ethan came at him. Iagan grabbed me, sheathing his claws and spun around, trying to move me out of danger's way while Ethan altered his path to avoid hurting me. Ethan grabbed the nearest tree and spun around it to release his momentum and then hissed at me.

"Are you insane?" Iagan asked me as he stood up and checked me for wounds.

"You have no right to interfere in our fight," Ethan snarled as he walked towards me.

I was very aware that I was naked right now, but I could do nothing about it at the moment unless I switched forms and for some reason I was too tired to do that right away.

"This is not the right time," I said. "I do not want you two to fight."

"We must fight," Iagan said. "It is the only way for us to determine who should rightfully be your mate."

"Why are you protecting him?" Ethan and Iagan asked at the same time.

I forced my body to switch forms again and ran away from them despite how cowardly I knew it was. *"I do not want you two to fight right now. Please."*

Ethan sighed. "It will happen eventually, Ainsley. It is only a matter of time."

"Come back," Iagan called and then switched forms, charging after me. *"Ainsley, come back and talk to me."*

I ignored them both, running as fast as I could into the forest. I needed space and time to think. I needed time to think about why I felt protective not only of Iagan, but of Ethan as well. Was there some truth to this Ra and Sekhmet thing?

I climbed up a tree and laid down on a branch. Why was this happening to me? I finally found a free male, but then Ethan, a Ra, shows up and complicates matters. Then I find out that my dad isn't even my biological father. Why hadn't my mom told me before? It did not change what I thought about my dad, but it did make me curious about my biological father. What had he been like? And why had my mom been so emotional when she went to talk to my dad? I needed to talk to her about it soon, but not right now. I did not need anything else added to my plate.

I scratched the tree with my claws, raking large claw marks into it. These stupid human girls had it so easy, especially Camille. If only Camille knew how easy she had it.

Dad roared from the house, summoning me home. I did not want to go. I did not want to face Ethan or Iagan and try to explain why I had interfered, because I was not really sure myself. Sadly, I had no choice in the matter, but to obey my alpha. I leapt down from my tree and walked through the forest towards my father and the two males who were courting me. Something moved to my left, but I paid it no mind because I was the largest hunter in these woods and had nothing to fear here.

It moved again and this time I realized it was big. Was it Lucy trying to play a trick on me? I pretended not to notice and continued on my way. I weaved around trees, using them to glance back occasionally and search for the thing stalking me.

A noise to my right. I stopped and stared towards it. Something was stalking me. Was it Ethan? Or Iagan? Or mom? I inhaled just as a breeze blew and smelled wolf. I charged forward, ready to fight it, but there was nothing there. Had I imagined it? I looked around, searching for the intruder and coming up unsuccessful.

I turned and started to walk away when I noticed a paw print in the dirt. It was old, but it was definitely a wolf's print. I looked towards the house and felt a chill go up my spine as I saw straight into my bedroom. Had someone been watching me last night?

How had a wolf gotten onto our land? I roared for my dad, trying to convey my urgency, and circled the paw print to look for others. I came up empty handed though. Dad ran to me in his human form and looked at me quizzically.

"What?" he asked.

I lifted my paw and pointed towards the wolf's paw print on

the ground. He squatted down by it and growled loudly. "How did a wolf make it this far into our territory?"

I growled in response to him.

"Go get the other males," Dad said. "Tell them we've been breached. And do not mention this to either Ethan or Iagan." I already knew not to tell non-pride members when there were issues in our pride. They could take it as a sign of weakness, and Dad did not need anyone challenging him right now.

I obeyed, running towards the other houses on our property, roaring as I approached. Martin and Steven both came out of their houses and met me in the middle. "We've been breached by a wolf," I told them.

Steven and Martin looked at each other and then back at me. "Are you sure?" Martin asked. He was in his thirties, a total geek, and very weak.

I looked at him and said, "Of course I am. Go see alpha. He is thirty feet from the house on the southwest side."

Steven had skin the color of dark chocolate, which matched his fur perfectly. He was tall, incredibly muscular, and was a very kind-hearted person. He lived with us because he did not have the meanness necessary for some parts of the alpha position, and I did not think he would be able to kill a pride member if he was supposed to. He kept to himself, except for occasional pride hunts which he would participate in to keep his position in the pride. I played with him quite frequently because he was a lot of fun and usually let me win in play fights.

They ran off without any further questions. I made my way to the house with thoughts of a warm shower and a bath on my mind. As I approached the house my hopes were shattered because both Ethan and Iagan were standing at the house, arguing.

I walked over to them and sat on my haunches. They stopped arguing and looked at me expectantly, but I just stared at them, waiting for someone to speak.

Ethan finally broke. "You must make a decision," he said angrily.

"Afraid of a little competition?" Iagan asked cockily.

Wasn't Ethan the one who was usually cocky? Why the sudden flip in attitude?

"Listen, cub, I'm refraining from ripping out your throat because she asked us not to fight right now. If you really want to die, we can set a date and time for your funeral," Ethan said.

Ah, there was the Ethan attitude.

I'm not making any decisions right now. I hardly know either of you. I will court you both until I decide which one I will take as my mate, I said in a matter of fact tone. Ethan and Iagan both started to say something, but I growled at them, making them stop talking. *That is not up for debate. If you don't like it than you can leave.* I waited with anxiousness, expecting Iagan to leave.

"Fine," Iagan said. "But, we have to come up with a plan of some sort. I do not want him around while I am trying to spend time with you."

"Agreed," Ethan said. "Why don't we alternate days? You can have her Tuesday, Thursday and Saturday."

"Why do you get her four days and I only get her three days?" Iagan asked. "That's not fair."

"Nothing is fair," Ethan snarled.

You both get me three days and I get a day to myself. I'm going to need time to decompress, I'm sure.

"That sounds fair enough," Iagan said. "Except I won't be able to stay up here too much longer."

"You both get the next two weeks to court her," Dad said as he walked towards us. "Two weeks is the normal period of courtship for females. After that she will make her decision. You will start the courting on Monday to give each other a fair amount of days with her." He looked down at me. "Understand?"

I bobbed my head once and then looked at the guys. *Ethan gets Monday, Wednesday and Saturday. Iagan gets Tuesday, Thursday and Friday. Sunday will be my free day. You can work out the other arrangements with my alpha."* I walked towards the door and Ethan pushed it open for me. *"Thank you."*

I walked down the hall and to the bathroom, shifting forms as soon as I got inside. I laid on the floor a moment to recover my energy. Why was I so tired? Maybe I had not slept well last night. The tile was cold against my bare skin and after a little while, it became too cold so I reluctantly stood up, closed the bathroom door and started the shower.

Today had definitely been a strange day. I was glad that things had been resolved without Iagan and Ethan fighting though. Not that I was looking forward to courting both of them. Especially since I knew I pretty much *had* to choose Ethan. How was this fair? I needed to talk Ethan into just letting me choose who I wanted and if, when, it ended up being Iagan, then he would have to accept it and just leave my pride alone. Ethan did not seem the type to agree to such a thing though.

I sighed. I knew myself well enough to know that even as horrible as an arranged marriage would be, I would do it to protect my pride. Even if this was not technically an arranged marriage, it would essentially be the same thing if I was forced to mate with him to protect my pride. I stepped into the hot shower and let the water wash away all of the negative feelings that were swirling around inside of my body and brain. This was probably the last time I would get to fully relax and I intended to enjoy it.

"Ainsley, we need to talk," Mom said through the bathroom door.

I groaned. So much for relaxing. "Okay. Let me finish washing first."

"Meet me in your father's study."

I soaped up and rinsed my hair and body and then dried off quickly. What did she want to talk about? I hoped it wasn't a birds and bees talk. I really did not need that talk again. I wrapped the towel securely around myself and ran from the bathroom to my room to get dressed. I had a bad feeling about this talk. Did it have to do with Dad telling me that he wasn't my biological father? Maybe Mom was just going to talk to me about my biological father so I could know a little about him. I got dressed in sweatpants and a baggy shirt and walked to my father's study.

I could hear Mom and Dad whispering to each other, but couldn't make out what they were saying. I knocked lightly on the door and then opened it, walking to the empty chair next to my Mom's and facing my Dad. "What's up?"

Mom took a deep breath and said, "Your father tells me that he finally told you the truth?"

"Yes, that he isn't my biological dad."

"How do you feel about that?" she asked with worry in her voice and tension holding her body rigid in the chair beside me.

I shrugged. "Dad is still my dad. Besides, the other guy is dead so it's not like I can go search him out and talk to him. Not that I want to or would want to, but I'm just saying it really doesn't change anything for me."

"So you aren't upset with me?" she asked.

It wasn't her fault that dad challenged him and took her. "Of course not. Why would I be mad? I mean I am a little irritated that it took you guys this long to tell me, but it doesn't really matter."

She exhaled in relief. "Good. There's something else I need to tell you."

Uh oh. This was not going to be good.

"I'm leaving," she said seriously.

"Where?" I asked. "For how long?" She never went anywhere, especially not without me.

"You're a woman now, Ainsley. You will be choosing a mate and once you turn eighteen you will be leaving this pride. I stayed because you love Aldric and he was a good father to you, but—"

"But you are not happy here," I answered for her.

She nodded. "I have tried, but I do not like being third in line."

I could understand that. "Where will you go?" I asked. I knew I was going to be venturing out on my own, but it was strange to think that I would not see my mom when I came to visit here.

"I have petitioned a pride in the town where I was raised. They are run by my brother, and he has agreed to allow me to join. It's in Nevada."

Nevada was a long drive from here. "Will I see you again?" I asked her. "Do you want to see me?" Maybe she was embarrassed that she had me. She had never acted embarrassed, but maybe that's why she wasn't emotional around me.

She hugged me. "Of course I want to see you. You are welcome to visit anytime. I actually know your uncle would love to meet you."

I hugged her back and whispered, "I'm going to miss you."

She took my chin between her thumb and pointer finger and lifted it until our eyes met. "Be strong. Only the strongest cubs can survive in this world."

"I'm the strongest cub there is," I said, finishing the phrase we said to each other when times were tough. "When are you leaving?"

"Tonight," she said. "I want to get to my brother's as soon as possible."

"Tonight?" I asked in shock. "What if I need you?" I had a huge decision ahead of me and now my mother wouldn't even be here to talk to me about it and help me.

"You can call me anytime, day or night and I will talk with you." She glanced at my dad and then stared into my eyes. "Make the right decision for you, Ainsley. Be the queen I know you are." She kissed my forehead and walked away, closing the door behind her.

I stared at the door and felt numb. Part of me knew I should feel happy for my mom because she was moving somewhere better for her. However the other, louder, part of me felt betrayed and sad.

Dad wrapped his arms around me and whispered, "I am still here, little cub. I will be here as long as you need me."

I turned around and buried my face into his chest to hide the tears in my eyes. "I am so confused right now. So many things are happening and changing. I just don't know what to do."

He pet my hair, purring softly. "You will take it one day at a time and make one decision at a time. No one is rushing you to choose today."

"What if I choose wrong?" I asked softly.

He laughed softly. "I have not ever known you to choose wrong. Whatever choice you make will be the right one for you. Even when you choose to do something that you were punished for later, you never regretted your actions because you had a valid reason in your opinion for doing it. I know you will do the same in regards to these males."

"Two weeks is not that much time to get to know a man and choose him to be your mate the rest of your life."

He pushed me back and said, "Not by human standards, but it is enough time for you to determine who will be able to protect you the best and who can provide the best life for you."

"Humans have it so easy," I complained in a whiny tone.

He laughed. "I know, sweetheart, but I also know that you are up for the challenge. You are a queen in werelion standards and you must act like one. It sucks being an adult, but there are perks later."

"If only I could skip straight to the perks," I said wistfully.

He laughed again and hugged me. "Go get some rest. You're going to be very busy these next two weeks."

I groaned and walked towards the door. "Don't remind me."

"Little cub," he called, using his nickname for me, as I reached for the door handle.

I turned to face him. "Yeah?"

"I love you."

I smiled. "I love you, too, Dad."

I walked to my room and laid down on my bed, burying my face in my pillow to stifle my crying. I didn't like to cry, but I was overwhelmed with emotions. I wrapped my blankets around myself and cried myself to sleep, letting all of my emotions out. Tomorrow I would put on my tough girl persona and I would be the lioness I was supposed to be and handle my problems one day at a time. Thank goodness I did not have to have the first date until Monday.

CHAPTER SIX

COLLEGE WAS FRUSTRATING BECAUSE MY GROUP STILL HAD NOT decided what group of gods we were going to work on. I finally told them that we were doing the Egyptian gods and they just had to deal with it. If I had not made the decision, we still would have been arguing over which gods to do instead of each having a god assigned to us to work on. It had already been one week and they had not made a decision. It was ridiculous. I chose Sekhmet as my assigned god, partially so that I could do some research for myself, and partially because I liked being able to present information to the class about someone I was a descendent of without them knowing.

We promised to email each other with the two-page typed descriptions of our assigned gods by tomorrow night so that Emily, one of the girls in the group, could print them out and work on a poster board. As I walked towards the bus stop, my car in the shop for something my dad wouldn't explain, I saw a familiar male, standing with his hands in his pockets and with a smirk on his face. I had to admit that Ethan was *very* attractive and totally had the bad boy persona going for him.

"Hello," I said with a smile as I stopped a few feet away from him. I had decided this morning that I was going to give him the same chance that I was giving Iagan. It was not fair for me to demonize him when it was not his fault that he had bad timing. If I had not met Iagan the weekend before, then things would have been a lot different when Ethan stopped to talk to me.

"Hello, Ainsley. How are you today?"

"I'm good," I said as I walked towards the bus stop.

"Would you like a ride so you don't have to take the bus?" he asked.

"Hmm," I said. "I don't know."

He laughed softly. "Come on."

I followed him to his motorcycle and put the spare helmet on. "So, why come pick me up?" I asked him. "Tonight is your night anyways."

He sat on the bike, and I sat down behind him, looping my fingers through his belt loops to hold on. "I wanted to see you," he said. "Contrary to what you think, I actually am genuinely interested in you becoming my mate."

"I bet you say that to all the single females you meet," I said somewhat seriously.

He shook his head. "You really need to learn more about me."

"That's what we are supposed to do tonight," I reminded him.

He started the engine and asked, "What type of food would you like to eat tonight? I was thinking Mexican."

We exited the college parking lot, and I leaned closer to him, pressing myself against his back. "Mexican sounds great," I said loud enough for him to hear me over the motor.

"Would you like to drive so your hair does not get messed up?" he asked.

I smiled because I had just been thinking about that. "Yes. You can just meet me at the house and then I will drive."

We stopped talking, and I enjoyed being near him. His scent smelled great. Why was his scent so different from Iagan's? Did it have to do with him being a Ra? I needed to remember to ask him tonight about it and if he knew anything about us. Was this feeling of security when I was with him due to it? Or was it because of how dominant he was? I wished I had had more time to look at him and assess him when he was in his warrior form, but I had been a little preoccupied trying to keep him and Iagan alive.

He stopped at the school and shut off the engine. "Safe and at school," he said with a smile.

I took off the helmet and handed it to him, feeling déjà vu at this having happened a week before. Had it only been a week? Had so much happened so quickly?

"Thank you for the ride," I said.

He smiled. "Anytime. I will see you tonight."

I leaned down and kissed his cheek, inhaling his powerful scent. "Bye."

The shocked look on his face was totally worth it. "Bye."

I walked away before he could recover and headed towards class. I would never admit it to anyone, but I was nervous and looking forward to our date tonight. What was I going to wear? Should I wear a dress? Or something low cut?

"Ainsley!" Theresa said loudly from beside me.

I turned and almost growled at her. "What?"

"I said your name three times and you ignored me. What are you thinking about that has you so distracted?" she asked as she folded her arms across her chest and tried to hide the fear I could sense from the rapid beating of her heart.

"Sorry, I have a date tonight and I was trying to figure out what I should wear," I said as we walked inside the classroom.

"Oh yeah? Is it with that hunk on the motorcycle?" she asked with a smirk. "If not then you should rethink your type."

I laughed. "Yes, it is with him. He isn't really my type though."

"So, sexy, ruggedly handsome men are not your type? Don't tell me you like nerds or something," she said mockingly.

"No, but apparently you do," I teased her.

She blushed. "Hey, we are not talking about me."

"Where is Felix?" I asked. "He never misses school."

"He's sick," she told me. "Some crazy dog bit him and he had to get rabies shots and so his mom let him stay home."

"That sucks," I said. I could not imagine getting bitten by a dog. Dogs were terrified of us because they knew we were predators. Plus, if a dog even tried to bite me I would tear its head off.

"Today I have decided," the teacher said as he walked to the front of the classroom, "that I do not feel like teaching. So, as long as you stay inside the classroom and don't break anything, you can do whatever you want."

"Yes!" all of the students exclaimed together. The teacher sat down and the room was instantly filled with talking.

"So, where is the sexy motorcycle man taking you on your date tonight?" Theresa asked.

"He said we were going to eat Mexican food, but aside from that I have no idea. I don't know what to wear tonight either," I complained.

"Well, it sort of depends on where you are going. If you are going to a nice Mexican place then you could wear a dress, but if you are going to a cheap place then I would just wear regular clothes," she said.

My cell phone vibrated and I took it out of my pocket. "I guess I will just have to ask him where we are going before I get ready." It was a text message from Iagan. Was this technically cheating on his part if he texted me on days that were not specified for him?

"How are you? I miss you."

"Is that him messaging you?" Theresa asked.

"No, it's someone else," I mumbled as I replied to him.

"I'm good. And flattery only gets you a fifth of a bonus point."

"Two boys?" Theresa asked. "Dang girl, you are busy."

"Only a fifth of a point? I guess I will have to increase the number of times I tell you that you are beautiful."

He was good at flattery. Not that that mattered in the long run, but it was nice to have someone saying nice things to me.

"Maybe you will have to show me tomorrow when I see you."

"I do not really want to talk about it. It's not as great as it sounds," I said. If only she knew.

"How can two guys not be great?" she asked in shock. "You are so weird."

"Let's just say that one of them is basically an arranged marriage type of thing but the other isn't. So, basically, I have to find a way to get out of the one to keep the other, but now I am not even sure which one I like," I admitted to her. I instantly regretted it though.

"Arranged marriage? What is this, the eighteen hundreds? I thought that was not done anymore? Or at least not done by most families anymore."

"I didn't think so either, but apparently I am in that predicament. I am hoping it is going to work out. My dad said he is thinking about letting me choose, but I have to seriously give it some thought and… Never mind I have said way too much."

She laughed. "I am glad I am not you."

"Dang, that's hurtful," I said. "So, what is going on with you and Felix?" I asked to change the subject.

"He is super nice and really sweet, but it's not like I can bring him home to meet my family. My dad would flip out." She shook her head. "Besides, I really can't see us lasting that long anyways. He wouldn't know how to handle himself around most of my family. They're a little crazy sometimes."

"I know how that is," I said with a laugh. "There's a reason I never invite any one over to my place."

"I'm still going to give it a shot," she said softly. "Maybe he will end up changing my mind down the road."

"You never know, he could be the nerdy Casanova," I said, wiggling my eyebrows.

She laughed and shook her head at me. "You are so weird sometimes."

If only she knew how jealous of her I was. She could date Felix for years and then decide that he wasn't right for her and dump him. I had to choose within two weeks and then there was no turning back. I would be stuck with whoever I chose for the rest of my life, or his life, if he ended up getting killed.

I tried to pay attention to my teachers, but my mind continued to wander to Ethan and Iagan. My mind mainly wandered to Ethan and what he was really like when he wasn't playing tough guy in front of others. Being raised by a man who was a killer if necessary, or a cuddler if the option arose, made me understand that men were not always what they appeared.

When I arrived home, my heart sped up at the sight of Ethan's motorcycle in the driveway beside my car. It was our first date, and I was really looking forward to it even though I would not admit that to anyone. I walked down the rest of the driveway, and Ethan walked to meet me, taking a place at my side.

"Hello," he said. "How was school?"

"Boring," not that I remembered much of my day since I had been daydreaming. "How was your day?"

"Productive. So, do you need to change or are you ready to go?" he asked as we headed towards the house.

"I need to change. What type of restaurant are we going to?" I asked as I opened the front door.

"It's a somewhat nice restaurant," he said motioning at himself.

I hadn't even looked at what he was wearing, having only stared at his face. Now that I looked, I realized that he was dressed in black slacks and a dark blue shirt that hugged his chest and showed the lines of his biceps. Man, he was hot.

"Okay then I need thirty minutes to get ready," I said, swallowing the drool inside my mouth that was trying to get out.

"Very well, I will wait for you in your father's study," he said, walking towards my dad's office.

What did they talk about in there? Or did they just sit in tense silence, staring at each other? I could picture my dad just staring at him, trying to make him uncomfortable, but then again I could also picture Ethan meeting Dad's gaze and giving him that stupidly sexy smirk of his. I walked to my room and changed into a blood red, low cut dress which had a rose on the hip and was very sexy. I grabbed the matching two inch high heels and slipped them on. My hair was already loosely curled and had survived the bike ride to school, so I just had to fix a couple frazzled hair pieces, and then add a little eye makeup, a necklace with a wolf's claw that I had taken in a fight that I had attached to a red leather cord to match the dress and I was ready.

I walked to the study and adjusted my dress, preparing to knock on the door. My cell phone vibrated as I raised my hand, so I stopped and pulled it out to read the message.

Iagan: *I can't wait to see you tomorrow.*

For some reason, it actually bothered me that he was texting me when he knew that I was supposed to be on my date with Ethan. I started to reply and Ethan asked, "I thought we were only supposed to speak or be with you on our specified days? Or do those rules only apply to me?"

I turned my phone around and showed him what I was texting. "Read it."

Me: *Can't talk, busy with Ethan on our date. See you tomorrow.*

He smirked. "I'm sorry. I just assumed—"

"You know what happens when you assume, right? It makes you look like an ass to me," I said with my own smirk.

Ethan picked up my hand and kissed the back of it softly, just a light caress of his lips and whispered, "I'm sorry. Will you forgive me?"

How could I say no to that serious and gorgeous face? "Since you apologized, then I guess I will accept your apology, but don't let it happen again," I said and he gave me a full smile back. It was the first full smile I had seen on him and it looked great.

"Shall we?" he asked, holding out his bent elbow.

Even though I didn't really have a choice to begin with, now I knew that taking his hand and going outside would begin our first date. Was I ready? Did it matter?

I reached out and laid my hand on the crook of his arm. A thrill went up my spine and a smile spread across my face. "Yes, let's go."

He walked to the front door and opened it for us. I stepped outside and saw eyes in the trees to the right watching us. I tried to see who it was, but could not figure out who it was. Was it Dad? Or was Iagan here, watching us?

"What are you looking at?" Ethan asked, looking in the same direction as me. He inhaled loudly and said, "I can't smell anyone."

I turned back towards the trees and the eyes were gone. Had I imagined it? Was I just being paranoid because of the paw print? "I thought I saw something, but I guess not."

"You want me to go investigate?" he asked.

Did he think I was scared? If I wanted to investigate I would do it myself. I wasn't some scared cub. "No, let's go." I walked to my car and as I unlocked the door, I glanced back at the woods, but of course there was nothing there.

I drove to Caballo Blanco, the best Mexican food in town, and parked the car in the lot, which was filled. I really hoped we would get seated quickly because I was starving. I started to open my door, but Ethan quickly moved from his seat, out of the car and around to my door, pulling it open and extending his hand for me to use it to step out of the car. I took his hand and let him pull me up, straightening my dress as I did.

"You look even more beautiful tonight," he whispered as he pulled me closer to him.

"You clean up nice, yourself," I said with a smirk.

He gave me his famous smirk back. "It's more fun to get dirty though, isn't it?"

I wasn't sure what he meant by that, but I wasn't going to let him rattle me so early on our date.

"I don't think you could handle how dirty I like it," I whispered and then walked away from him towards the front door of the restaurant.

"You don't know until you try," he said behind me as he walked to catch up to me. I laughed and waited at the door for him to open it. He walked around me and opened the door, stepping back so I could walk in in front of him. "Ladies first," he said.

I stepped in and inhaled the spicy aroma that filled the restaurant. Mariachi music played in the background, just loud enough to be heard over the talking of the patrons. Most of the booths were filled and the waiters moved quickly from one to the next, taking orders and refilling drinks as fast as they could.

Ethan asked for a table for two, and the hostess immediately grabbed menus and headed towards the back of the room. I followed behind the hostess with Ethan behind me. Women paused to look at him, and I felt proud that I was with him and jealous that they were even looking at him. It was very strange because I had never dealt with those emotions before.

"Your waiter will be with you soon," the hostess said and then hurried back to the front to seat more people.

"I'm glad they sat us quickly. I'm starving," I said as I picked up the menu and tried to figure out what entrée I wanted. If I could, I would have ordered one of everything.

"Would you like something to drink besides water?" a Hispanic man in his thirties asked as he set chips, salsa and glasses of water down on the table.

"Iced tea," I said with a smile and then resumed looking at my menu.

"Water is fine for me," Ethan said. The waiter walked away and Ethan asked, "Do you know what you want?"

"Everything," I mumbled as I chewed on a chip. "I think I will have the enchiladas with red sauce. What are you having?" I asked and then closed my menu and set it down on the table to look at him.

His menu was already closed and face down on the table, and he was dipping a chip into the salsa. "I am going to have steak fajitas."

"What's your favorite meat?" I asked him.

"Beef," he answered right away. "Tri tip, filet mignon, skirt steak, ground. It's all delicious. You can't eat a bad piece of beef in my opinion."

"Beef is pretty good," I admitted, grabbed a chip and dipped it into the salsa. I popped it into my mouth, and immediately reached for another. They were delicious.

"What's your favorite?" he asked as he leaned back against his chair, looking like he should have been a king on a throne instead of a male werelion in a restaurant.

"Goose," I said with a smile. "Didn't see that answer coming did you?"

He shook his head and smiled just enough to tilt up the corners of his mouth. "No, I did not. Then again I did not see you coming either."

I laughed a short laugh. "I should be the one saying that about you. You found me, not the other way around."

"True," he said with a light chuckle. "Why were you so adamant about not letting me court you in the beginning?" he asked, leaning forward slightly.

I decided to be honest with him because I needed to hear his honest answer. "I was already being courted by Iagan, plus, you look like a typical alpha and a typical alpha has many mates."

"And that's bad?" he asked curiously.

"I don't want to be one of a male's harem of mates. I know it's not a typical werelion attitude, but I want to be with a mate that only needs me as a mate, not three or four others. I don't want to be pushed to the side or forgotten about." It had always bothered me that the males had multiple mates, when there were less females anyways. Shouldn't we have been the ones with our own harem?

He sat in stunned silence and absorbed what I had said. He opened his mouth to say something, but our waiter returned and interrupted him.

"Have you both decided?" the waiter asked as he set my iced tea on the table.

"Yes," Ethan said. "The lady would like three *enchiladas rojas* and I would like steak fajitas."

"I'll be right back with refills for your waters. Thank you." He picked up the menus and left.

I grabbed a chip and scooped salsa on to it, waiting nervously for Ethan's response. "You still haven't asked me the question you have been wanting to," he said. "Why is that?"

How did he know? "I'm nervous about your answer I suppose," I said as I chewed on the chip and enjoyed the spicy salsa. "What pride did you come from?" I asked to change the topic.

"That's not the question you wanted to ask me," he said. I stared at him and he sighed. "I was in my uncle's pride until two months ago. Both of my parents have died in battles and I left to search for a mate."

"Are you willing to let me go to college?"

"Of course. You are welcome to do whatever you would like, that is within reason, once we are mates," he said.

"Are you willing to go on a trip out of the country with me once I graduate?"

"Where to?" he asked. "Rome? France? London?"

"All of them," I said with a smile. "Everywhere."

"We would need a month to travel," he said. "Are you willing to miss out on school for traveling?"

"We can travel over the summer," I said. "Where do you want to live?"

"In a house, with you," he answered.

"In the city?" I asked.

He laughed and shook his head. "What lion would want to live surrounded by humans? No, we would live in the mountains with plenty of room to run."

"What do you want to do for work?" I asked.

"I am the vice president of my uncles' business. I travel around and inspect the businesses and talk with the employees to ensure they are being treated equally."

I sat there and digested all of his answers. He sounded too good to be true.

"Are you going to ask the real question you have been wanting to ask me?" he asked me softly.

I exhaled. I needed to ask him and just get it over with. "Do you have other mates?"

"Was that so hard?" he asked me with a soft smile.

"Yes. Will you answer the question?"

"I will," he said, but then the server came with our food and saved him from having to say anymore.

If I hadn't been so hungry, I would have pressed him for an answer, but I let him sit smugly as he ate. The food was delicious and I was very glad that he had ordered three enchiladas for me instead of the two that I would have normally ordered. I generally tried to keep up human appearances, but then I ended up eating more when I got home.

I finished eating and leaned back, drinking my iced tea and watching Ethan. He finished his food a couple of minutes later and looked back at me. "Are you ready to go?" he asked.

I nodded and stood, smoothing my dress and walking ahead of him towards the front of the restaurant. I pushed open the door just as a man was walking inside, causing us to collide. His scent enveloped me, making me gag. Werewolf. I stepped back from him, but he grabbed my arm and growled in my face.

I tensed, ready to push him out of the restaurant so we could fight. He was at least six and a half feet tall with shoulders so broad he almost blocked the entire doorway. He had on a grey suit and a black tie that did not match. He was the type of guy that no human would even make a comment to about the fact that his outfit did not match.

Ethan stepped forward and placed his hand on the wolf's wrist. "Excuse us. You are blocking the door," he said with a dangerously low voice.

"You should watch where you're going," the wolf said to me, completely ignoring Ethan. "Next time, I won't be so forgiving."

"Who said I wanted your forgiveness?" I snarled.

He looked down at my necklace, and his lip twitched upwards in a snarl. "You think you're real tough, don't you girl?"

"Release her arm before I break yours," Ethan growled. "This is my only warning to you."

"Soon enough, girl. You will get what's coming to you soon enough," the wolf said and then released my arm, trying to walk past us into the restaurant.

Ethan stepped into his path though, refusing to let him by. "What was that supposed to mean? Are you threatening her?"

The wolf looked at Ethan like he had just seen him for the first time. "Not a threat, tiger, just a statement of fact."

Tiger? Really that was the insult he was going with? Pathetic.

"Excuse me," a little old woman said behind us with a thick Spanish accent. "Can you please move out of the doorway?"

The wolf stepped sideways and smiled at her. "Of course, ma'am."

Ethan nudged my lower back with his hand, urging me outside. I obeyed, not wanting to get the little old lady involved in our fight.

What did that wolf mean by his threat? He was not the one who had been on the bus with me or the one who had been at the house. Why were there so many different wolves interacting with me all of a sudden? Did it have something to do with Ethan coming here?

"Would you like me to drive?" he asked, drawing my attention back to him.

"Sure," I said, handed him my keys, and walked to the passenger door. I was impressed with his fearless attitude towards the wolf, but I wondered if it had been a show or if he really would have fought the wolf to protect me.

We got inside the car and he started the engine, driving away from the restaurant. "Are you alright?" he asked me.

I laughed. "I'm sorry. I'm being a terrible date. I'm fine. I was just wondering what the wolf meant by what he said."

"Do not even worry about it. He was just being a jerk. He knew that we could not do anything since there were so many humans around, so he was just taunting us."

Was he? If I told Ethan everything that had happened to me recently, would he still say the same thing? I almost told him, but I did not want him to think my pride was weak so I bit my tongue and looked out the window.

"Where are we going?" I asked as he pulled off the freeway and headed downtown.

"Well, I figured that we should put your pretty dress to use. Dinner was not enough to satisfy my view of you in that dress," he said with a sideways glance at me.

I kept quiet until he parked the car and unbuckled his seatbelt. "I am not going anywhere until you answer my question," I said and folded my arms over my chest. I could be stubborn when the occasion called for it.

He laughed. "I like it when you're feisty."

I continued to stare at him, not saying anything and not moving.

"Zero," he said, staring straight into my eyes to prove that he was not lying.

"Zero?" I asked. "Seriously?" I had expected at least two or maybe four.

He reached over and slid his hand across my cheek. "I have been waiting for someone like you. I was so excited when I smelled you, that I wanted to take you away right then."

"Zero?" I asked again. He had to be lying.

"I have zero mates and am only courting one female, you," he whispered as his face moved closer to mine.

"Thank you for answering the question," I said with a smile and in one swift motion I turned out of his hand and climbed out of the car. I heard him laugh softly inside the car and was pleased with myself. He climbed out, and I waited for him to lead the way since I had no clue where we were going.

He took my hand and led me down two blocks and then stopped at the end of a line of about ten people. "Just let me talk and you stand there and look pretty."

I would have taken offense to that, but I knew he was not trying to be demeaning, so I did as he asked and kept quiet, smiled, and leaned against him as he talked with the bouncer at the door. The bouncer looked at me and then opened the door, letting us inside. The instant the door opened, the stench of sweaty humans engulfed my nose and the loud music drowned out any other sounds. Ethan tugged on my hand gently, pulling me inside and into the mass of swaying, dancing bodies.

I had to sidestep several people as they danced without reservations and with no regard for anyone around them. Ethan pulled us into a somewhat open spot and turned around, wrapping his arms around my waist as he began to dance with me. It was my first time ever being inside of a dance club, and I took advantage of it because I loved to dance. I danced my heart out and was surprised at how good of a dancer Ethan was. I danced until I was so thirsty that I could barely open my mouth.

I tapped Ethan and then pointed at the bar. He thankfully understood and took my hand, leading me through the crowd and to the bar. "Two waters, please," he ordered. He turned to me and smiled. "Having fun?"

I nodded. "I love dancing."

"I thought you would." He glanced at his watch and sighed. "Sadly we must return you to your castle, Cinderella."

I looked at his watch and was shocked to see that it was already ten o'clock. Had we really been dancing for that long?

He took the water bottles from the bartender, handed her a twenty dollar bill and led me outside. I took long drinks of the bottle of water, enjoying the cold liquid running down my burning throat. We climbed into the car, and I sat in the passenger seat and finished my bottle. "Thank you," I said to Ethan as he started the car.

He smiled. "You are welcome."

He drove without talking, letting the radio songs fill the comfortable silence between us and letting me think about our date. He had behaved well and he had stuck up for me when that wolf threatened me. Overall it had been a good date. Not that I could make a decision about a permanent relationship based on one night, but it was a definite positive for him.

Part of me had really wanted to kiss him in the car earlier, but I did not want him getting any cockier than he already was. His ego did not need any inflation. Dancing had been a lot of fun, and I hoped that we could go again, maybe on our next date. I watched him out of the corner of my eye and really enjoyed the view. I knew that with him, I would be protected and I would never have to worry about my physical safety, but part of me was still worried about my emotional safety with him.

He parked in front of the house and shut off the car engine, sitting still as he looked out the window. "Your dad waited for you," he said with a smirk.

I looked in the direction he was and sure enough, Dad stood

on the front porch with his arms folded and a serious look on his face. Something was wrong, I could tell by the tenseness in his posture. "I better say good night," I said, turning to face him. I smiled. "I had a really good time tonight. Thank you."

"You're welcome. Since I can't stay, will you do me a favor?"

"Maybe," I said suspiciously.

He held out a cell phone, "Will you give me your phone number so I can text you?"

I took his phone, added my number to his contacts and then gave him back the phone. "There. Now I can ignore your texts tomorrow when I'm out with Iagan," I teased him.

He leaned over and kissed my cheek softly. "Good night, Ainsley. Thank you for the date. I look forward to our date in two days."

I smiled and whispered, "I'm looking forward to it as well." I climbed out of the car and watched as he walked to his motorcycle. "What's going on, Dad?" I asked as he walked towards me.

"A wolf was on our property again tonight," he said with lots of growl in his voice. "We could not catch him. We are on lockdown effective now."

"Lockdown?" I asked in shock. "I am not a child anymore. I can handle myself against a wolf."

"I am alpha here and you will obey my orders. Until we catch this wolf, I do not want you out alone. Do you understand?" he asked me.

He rarely acted so angry or used his title as alpha to order me around. "Okay." I walked towards the house, listening to the sound of Ethan's motorcycle driving away. I had not expected to enjoy tonight as much as I had. I really was looking forward to seeing him in two days.

I climbed into bed that night and dreamed of hunting with Ethan.

CHAPTER SEVEN

"Are you hungry?" Iagan asked as we headed towards his car for our date.

"I'm always hungry," I said half-jokingly and half-seriously. "Why?"

"I was thinking that we could go for a round of miniature golf before we ate," he said with a smile.

"Sure," I said. It did not sound as fun as going dancing, but I had not been miniature golfing in a long time. I climbed inside of his car and buckled my seat belt. I took a deep breath and pushed all thoughts of Ethan out of my head. In order to give them both an equal chance, I had to forget about the other and treat them like I was dating them individually. I wanted to be sure that I gave them all separate and equal chances to show to me who would be the best mate for me.

"I had a dream about you last night," he said as we drove to the arcade and miniature golf place called Excalibur.

"Oh? What happened in this dream?" I asked, feeling nervous at his response. Please don't let it be anything gross.

"We were walking down the street and some wolf attacked

you. We both changed and tore into the wolf like it was an antelope," he said with a smile.

I smiled back at him, enjoying the vision. "That sounds fun."

"Yeah," he said and then glanced at me. "Then you kissed me."

"Really?" I said in surprise. "Well maybe if you play your cards right, I might give you a kiss tonight."

"I'm looking forward to it."

I laughed and then asked, "So, do you want to continue our game of questions that we had started on our first date?"

He shrugged. "Okay. Whose turn is it?"

"Mine," I said quickly. "Where would you want to live if you could live anywhere?"

"Hmm," he said as he thought. "Probably somewhere where there were lots of trees. Plenty of room for us to hunt in without the humans seeing us."

That was sort of a boring response.

"What about you?" he asked.

"I would want to live in Greece or Rome or somewhere exotic," I said with a smile. "Of course, I won't be able to choose where I want to live until I can visit them all and decide from experience. I think I would really like Australia, too, though."

"Australia?" he asked, lifting a brow. "There aren't too many trees there."

"No, but there is a lot of open land where wild animals are, and I'm sure we could find areas to keep hidden." I thought a second and then said, "I guess I could live in the Amazon. There we could keep hidden from humans and take hold of the jungle, claiming it for ourselves. I've always wanted to meet a jaguar or leopard in person and see if they are frightened of us or if they would take to us."

"Wow, you have really thought about this," he said softly.

"What else am I supposed to do during school? Pay attention?" I laughed and he shook his head with a smile on his face. "My turn," I said as I tapped my chin in thought. "If you could turn into any other animal besides a lion, what would you choose?"

"Bear," he answered immediately. "They are big, smart, powerful, feared and revered."

I had met a couple werebears who had passed through and stopped to talk with my dad and they were not the smartest beings. Not that they were stupid, but they were not geniuses either.

"If you could change any human into a lion so that you could have them as a mate, who would you choose?" he asked.

"We can't turn humans into werelions." Really? Did he not know that?

"I know that," he said. "This is just a hypothetical question."

That was a hard decision to make. "Well, based just on looks I would probably choose Hugh Jackman."

"Really?" he said, "I would have thought that you would have chosen Liam Hemsworth or someone like him."

"Not my type," I said with a shrug. "Who would you choose?"

"Nina Dobrev," he said without hesitating.

I had to admit, she was very attractive. We pulled into *Excalibur* and made our way to the line of people waiting to buy a round of miniature golf. Guys checked me out as we walked by, and Iagan moved a step closer to me, trying to show that we were together. I gritted my teeth to keep from saying something to him about it. There should be no reason that he would need to prove that we were together or try to keep guys away from me. They were human, and I had absolutely no interest in them. Iagan behaving that way showed he was immature. Immature was not attractive.

We stood in line, and I watched the other teenagers laughing and having a good time together. I was trying to have a good time with Iagan, but even though he said he missed me or said he liked me, I could not feel it. The spark I had felt when I had met him at his pride's land was gone. Was it me?

Another guy checked me out as he walked by and smiled at me. I smiled back at him and then glanced at Iagan. He was glaring at the guy and walked a step closer to me, so close that our arms touched. The guy had already moved on, though so he did not even see it. I sighed. Had I matured more than I was aware of? Did I need a guy more mature than Iagan?

We got to the front of the line and Iagan asked me to pay half of the costs. I handed him the cash, and tried to stifle my anger. It wasn't that I thought guys had to pay every time a couple went on a date, but most werelion courting protocol said that guys paid for the dates. I had never heard of any females paying before.

I grabbed the golf club from the cashier and followed Iagan as he got two balls from the machine with the tokens we had been given. There were a lot of teenagers at Excalibur and when we made our way out to the first hole I sighed at the line that was already formed, waiting to start their turns. They had better hurry before I decided to use one of them as my appetizer.

"So, do you have any human friends at school?" Iagan asked.

"Yeah, I have two, but we don't hang out outside of school. Obviously, I could not bring them to my house." I laughed and shook my head. "That would be fun to watch, though."

"Any male friends?" he asked with a bit of jealousy evident in his tone.

"One, but he is a super nerd and my other friend is into him right now," I said. "There is one guy who is interested in me, but I've told him that I am not interested and that we are not a good match. He's the star football and basketball player for the school though and does not take no for an answer very easily."

"Has he touched you?" he asked in a clipped tone.

I laughed. "Do you really think I would let any human touch me that I did not want to? I am not the helpless little cub you saved from the wolf." My hand involuntarily moved up towards my scar and I forced it back down to my side.

Iagan moved closer to me, resting his hand on the back of my arm. "I know that. I just feel very protective of you. It has been eating me up inside thinking about you and what kind of trouble you might find yourself in with me so far away. Every night since then I have wondered what you were doing and if you were thinking about me. Did you think about me?"

"Occasionally," I admitted. "But then I blocked out that night, and I did not even remember. I don't know why I did that. I guess my mind thought it was too much for me to handle at the time and tried to suppress that memory as much as it could."

He moved his hand around so that it was around my back and whispered, "I missed you yesterday."

I smiled, but did not say anything. I could not admit to him that I did not miss him because I had been with Ethan. Tall, handsome and strong Ethan. What was he doing? Was he thinking about me?

"What's wrong?" he asked.

I shook my head. "Sorry, I was just thinking about my friend at school who has been out sick and thinking how I love that I do not get sick."

"It is a definite perk," he said with a nod.

"Oh, look. It's our turn," I said, putting my ball on the tee. "I'll go first." I focused on the hole ahead and hit the ball.

One hour later and I was walking away with a smile while Iagan was pouting because he had lost. "I can't believe you beat me," he said with a shake of his head.

"Girls are just better than guys at most things," I said cockily.

"Pfft."

"I bet I am faster than you," I said as we headed towards his car.

"Not a chance," he said.

"Fine, when we get to my place, I challenge you to a foot race," I said.

"What do I win when I beat you?" he asked with a smirk as he unlocked the doors.

"If you win, I will give you a kiss," I said.

He climbed inside and waited until I was buckled before asking, "And what if you win?"

"If I win you have to get me a gift."

"A gift?" he asked. "What kind of gift?"

I shrugged. "Whatever you think I will like. You cannot spend more than $20 and you have to bring it to our next date."

"Deal," he said holding out his hand for me to shake.

I shook it and then he started the car, heading to dinner. He talked about his pride and I tried to stay interested, but I really did not care about the pride that we would not be staying with. It did make me realize that I needed to find out more about Ethan and his pride. I reprimanded myself for thinking about Ethan again, and tried to pay more attention to Iagan.

We stood outside my house, and I pointed to the largest tree which was approximately one hundred yards away. "First person to touch the tree wins," I said.

He nodded and squatted down with one leg back in a prepared stance. "Ready?"

I assumed the same stance and said, "On your mark, get set—"

"Go!" he yelled as he took off, running ahead of me.

"Cheater," I called as I ran after him, running for all I was worth. I caught up to him and started to creep passed him.

"Oh, no you don't," he said as he increased his speed, catching up to me. We ran as fast as we could, shoulder to shoulder as we neared the tree.

I had to win. I could not let him win a kiss. I ran sideways, cutting him off and making him stumble as he tried to keep from tripping on me.

"Now, who's the cheater," he yelled as I ran ahead of him and touched the tree.

"Don't be a sore loser," I said with a bright smile as I caught my breath.

"Rematch," he said as he gasped for breath. "Dang, I am out of shape."

I laughed. "I could have told you that."

He snarled playfully. "I can still beat you in a fight."

I rolled my eyes. "How pathetic of a male would you be if you couldn't?"

"Ouch," he said as he clutched at his chest. "That was cruel."

I laughed and started heading back towards my house. "Well, it looks like you better go shopping tomorrow."

"Yeah, yeah," he grumbled. "I will figure something out."

I walked backwards up the steps and onto my porch. "Well, I guess I will see you in two days," I said.

"So, you are really not going to give me a kiss?" he asked. "Seriously?"

I shook my head. "Nope, you have to earn a kiss."

Something dark passed over his face, but it was gone so quickly that I thought I had imagined it, and then he smiled. "Okay. Good night, Ainsley."

I smiled. "Night."

I walked into the house and leaned against the door as soon as it was closed. There was something not quite right with him. It was like he was harboring some deep seeded anger that occasionally reared its head when I did something he did not like. Or was I just imaging that? I was probably imaging it.

I walked into my room and flopped down onto my bed, pulling my cell phone out to check if I had any messages. Zero. Part of me felt sad that Ethan had not messaged me while part of me knew that he was simply abiding by my wishes and the rules we had set in place.

I started to type him a message, but I immediately deleted it. What was I thinking?

"He hasn't been answering my calls or texts," Theresa complained the next day at lunch to me about Felix. "I'm starting to get worried that something is seriously wrong. Or maybe he just isn't into me and can't find the *cajones* to tell me."

"If he wasn't in to you, he would still be at school," I reminded her. "He must have the flu or something crazy. You know how sick you get when you have the flu." Not that I knew what that was like since I had never been sick.

"Yeah, you are probably right," she mumbled as she ate her burger.

"Hey, Ainsley," Chuck said with a bright smile. "How are you? I haven't seen you lately."

"Good," I said with a smile, "Just busy with college and my boyfriend."

"Boyfriend?" he asked. His smile wilted a little and he said, "Oh. Well if you ever want to hang out or anything you have my number."

"Will do," I said with a smile. "Later."

He walked away, and I could tell that he was a little upset that I had a boyfriend now. Not that I really did since I had two.

"Boyfriend?" Theresa asked. "Did you finally pick one?"

"No comment," I grumbled as I took a bite from my burger.

She laughed and shook her head. "You better pick one soon or they both might leave you."

If only it were that easy. I reached for my phone, but pulled my hand away from it. I had been waiting all day for Ethan to message me and he hadn't yet. He also had not visited me at college either. What was he doing?

I drug myself through the rest of the school day and then forced myself to go the speed limit as I drove home. Yes, I was excited to see Ethan. Perhaps, but I would never admit it. I parked my car and fought the rush of sadness I felt when I realized that Ethan's motorcycle was not there. I walked into the house and sniffed. No recent scents from Ethan. Where was he? My room was also empty so I sat down on my bed and pulled out my cell phone. It was his day so I had every right to text and ask when he was coming.

Me: *Hey. When will you be here?*

I set my cell phone down and tried to sidetrack myself with homework. It worked for about two minutes and then every thirty seconds I looked at the phone. Five minutes later I finally received a text message from Ethan.

Ethan: *Look out your window.*

I turned around and Ethan smiled at me from outside my window. I walked over with a smile on my face. He had come. I unlocked the window and then slid the bottom part of the window upwards. I hadn't had a screen on it since I was five and had started sneaking out to go run through the forest. Dad had stopped replacing them after the tenth one.

I leaned out and asked, "What are you doing out here?"

He was standing outside with his arms behind his back and a very smug smile on his face. "Have you been good today?" he asked.

I smirked. "It depends. Do I get something for being good or for being bad?"

He laughed. "This time you would get something for being good."

"Well, then I have been very *very* good," I said as I leaned further out of the window, using my elbows on the sill for balance.

He brought his arms forward and held out a bouquet of roses towards me. "I'm sorry I did not text you earlier today. I was running a couple of errands."

I took the roses and sniffed them. They smelled great. "Don't worry about it. Thank you for the roses," I said. "I should put them in water."

He leaned forward and said, "I missed you yesterday."

I smiled and leaned back out the window, moving my face closer to his. "If you had missed me, you should have texted me."

He stepped forward, closing the distance between us so that our faces were inches apart. "I told you, I was busy. I brought the flowers to apologize. I really did miss you."

"Prove it," I whispered.

He closed the distance and pressed his lips lightly against mine. "Hunt with me," he said more as an order than a request.

"Say please," I whispered and then kissed him on his lips one more time.

"Please," he whispered against my lips and then purred.

I pulled back and shut my window. He stood where he was, watching me. I tugged on the cord and my blinds dropped down, concealing me from his view. I stripped from my clothes and then giggled softly. I had finally kissed him. It wasn't the incredibly passionate kiss that I had really wanted, but it had still been a great kiss. I shifted forms as fast as I could and made my way out of the house. I looked for Ethan, but I could not see him. I lifted my snout and sniffed, testing the air for his scent. He was somewhere to the left.

I turned right, making my way around the house, hugging against it so only my left side was exposed. I turned around the house, passing underneath my dad's window and I heard a twig snap behind me. He was playing carelessly with me. I pretended not to hear it and continued on my way around the house. I turned around the next corner and then spun around, waiting for him to follow. I crouched down, ready to leap forward and waited. A good hunter could wait for hours if needed.

Something large landed on top of me. I spun around, trying to free myself and hissed loudly. I turned my head and Ethan pushed my face with his paw. I growled at him and he growled back.

"*I win*," he said.

"Never."

He leapt off of me and ran into the forest. I followed him, running as fast as I could, catching up to him and then leaping onto his back. He growled, and I wrapped my paws around him, holding on as he fell. *"I win."*

A deer ran out from behind a tree ahead of us. I followed it with Ethan right on my heels. Ethan leapt on its front shoulders, and I jumped onto its back. Ethan bit into its throat, killing it and we feasted. I ate until I was so full that I could not run and then laid down on the ground, licking my paws to clean them.

"Full?" he asked me as he laid down beside me and started cleaning his paws as well.

"Very full."

We cleaned ourselves and then he nudged me with his shoulder. *"Get dressed and meet me at the river."*

"Why?"

"To go swimming, duh." He said as he headed towards the river. *"Hurry."*

I walked back to the house and changed forms and then put on a bathing suit, wrapping a towel around myself. I jogged to the river on the outskirts of our territory and stopped twenty feet away. Ethan stood at the edge of the river with only a pair of swimming trunks on. He had a perfect body with abs that looked like they were carved from stone. He was gorgeous.

I recomposed myself and walked towards him. "Why the sudden urge to swim?" I asked. Not that I minded. I really liked the view of him in his swimming trunks.

He turned towards me with a smile on his face. "I like swimming."

I untied my towel and dropped it on the ground. Ethan looked from the towel on the ground, to my toes and slowly up my body. I walked towards him and then right past him, dipping my toes in the water. It was cold, but our higher body temperatures made it very relaxing. I walked into the water until it was up to my waist and then turned towards Ethan. "You coming?"

He walked into the river until he was beside me and then grabbed me and dunked us both under the water. He released me and I came up sputtering and wiping water out of my eyes. "Jerk."

He smiled. "I find it's always best to just jump in instead of letting yourself adjust to the water."

I splashed water at his face. "Right."

He splashed back at me and then jumped at me. I spun to the right, avoiding his arms. He was faster than I had expected though and spun around, grabbing me in a big hug with me facing him. "Caught you."

I struggled against his hold and then he kissed me. It was a deep kiss and exactly what I had wanted. I wrapped my legs around his waist as we floated in the water and my arms around his shoulders.

He pulled back and I smiled at him. "I missed you, too."

He smirked, giving me his cocky smile. "I know."

"You know?" I asked as I unwrapped myself from him.

He kept his arms around me and tightened his grip. "I bet you were wanting to text me earlier today, but you didn't because you were trying to play cool."

I shook my head since I could not speak and lie without him knowing.

He kissed my cheek and whispered, "I bet you were thinking about me yesterday while you were out with Iagan, too."

I shook my head. "I won't talk to you about my dates with Iagan and I won't tell him about ours."

"Good," he whispered against my neck, making me shiver. "Then you won't have to tell him about us kissing." He kissed me again, and I melted against him. It felt so right being with him. It felt right to kiss him where I did not think it would feel right kissing Iagan. Why?

I pulled away from the kiss and pushed away from him. "So,

what are we doing after our swimming session?" I swam out farther into the river, getting out so far that I could not touch the ground even when the water went up over my head. I kicked my legs slowly to keep afloat.

He followed me and began swimming in a circle around me. It reminded me of the first day I had met him when he was circling me at my college. "I was planning for us to go to a movie and then get some dessert."

Kisses from him were dessert enough. "That sounds good."

He reached for me, and I dodged, diving underneath the water and swimming back towards the shore. I surfaced only to have his arms grab me from behind and hold me against his chest. "You won't get away from me," he whispered into my ear. "I will always be able to find you."

Those simple words made me feel the safest I had ever felt before. I relaxed into his arms and whispered, "You always know what to say. Are you sure you don't have any other mates?"

"I promise that I do not have any mates."

I pulled out of his arms, needing to stop being so incredibly one-sided about my feelings. I needed to get to know him a little more before I made my decision. "What movie are we going to see?" I asked as I wrapped my towel around myself.

"There are a couple movies to pick from. One is a drama and one is an action movie."

"No chick flicks?" I asked with a smirk.

He smiled. "I would see anything that you wanted to, even a chick flick. I don't think that you are really a chick flick girl anyways."

"No, I am not. I think I am in the mood for an action movie."

"Alright, let's get to the house, get changed, and then we can head out," he said as he put his arm around my shoulders. "Then, I will take you to get dessert from wherever you want."

"I like the sound of that," I said and then leaned into him.

I was still going to go on the dates with Iagan, but I could not deny the connection I felt with Ethan.

"What if I find another mate?" I asked him.

"What?"

"What if I'm the one who finds an additional mate? Not Iagan, but another guy. Would you be okay with that?"

He thought about it a moment and said, "As long as I was your mate, and you didn't sideline me, then I would be fine with you having an additional mate. There are more males anyway. It would make sense for you to have multiple mates. I can't say I'm going to like him or be his friend, but I wouldn't leave you or despise you if you found another mate you loved."

Why was he so perfect?

"Just so we're clear, you couldn't have another mate," I said.

He smirked. "I'm aware of your double standard and I accept it."

He accepted it, but I knew for certain that Iagan wouldn't.

This just furthered my connection with Ethan.

CHAPTER EIGHT

IAGAN AND I WERE SITTING AT A CHINESE FOOD RESTAURANT ON our date when I smelled wolf. It was not the scent of any of the wolves that I had encountered before. I scanned the restaurant, trying to be as discreet as possible, but I did not see anyone who looked familiar or anyone who seemed interested in me. Why were so many different wolves coming into this area? They usually stayed away because they knew our pride was here, only coming occasionally for necessary trips. What had changed? Was I just being paranoid about them being around me?

"So, what are your plans for your day off?" Iagan asked as he picked up a piece of broccoli with his chopsticks.

"I am going to sit inside the house and watch TV all day." Since I was on lockdown and couldn't go anywhere except the necessaries and with Iagan and Ethan. Dad said he felt that I was safe enough with Iagan and Ethan that he would allow me to go on our dates still. Plus, the fact that Dad did not want the guys to find out that we were having wolf problems and think that my dad was incapable of protecting his pride.

"Sounds boring," he said with a laugh. "I could come over and keep you company," he offered as he wiggled his eyebrows.

I definitely did not want to deal with him tomorrow. He had become increasingly cocky over the past two dates, and it was really getting on my nerves. "I'll pass," I said with a smile. "What are you going to be doing?" Not that I really cared.

"I'm going to go visit my pride. I've been away from them for a while and need to check in with them in person." He reached across the table and slid his hand underneath mine. "I'm going to miss you, though."

I was glad that I had this break from them both. I needed a day to really think about the dates and try and figure out why I was feeling so negatively about Iagan. I had originally been sure that I was going to choose him and now I felt the opposite.

"Would you two care for any dessert?" our waiter asked.

"No, thank you," I said with a smile. "Can we have our check please?"

He set it on the table and smiled back at me, "Of course."

"I'm sorry that my dad pushed my curfew up so far. He has been acting very protective lately," I said with an apologetic smile at Iagan.

He took out cash and put it inside the bill's folder. "Don't worry about it. I'm happy that I get to court you in the first place."

We stood and headed towards the exit. "I'm glad, too. I enjoy spending time with you." We walked to his car, and I climbed inside. "How are your classes going?" I asked him.

He shrugged. "I haven't gone in a while. I think I'm going to drop out."

"Why?" I asked, incredibly shocked that he would drop out of college. "What are you going to do instead?"

"I've been thinking about opening a repair shop, you know, for vehicles. I like working on cars and I think it would be fun," he said with a smile.

"Really?" I asked, not at all surprised that he would want to do something that would be the only thing he did for the rest of his life. Could I be a mechanic's wife? What would our lives be like if I decided that I wanted him as a mate? It seemed boring and like I would never be able to travel. Would I want to be stuck in the same town for the rest of our lives? Some humans craved that, but I could not envision myself living at the same town and finding some mundane job to do while he worked as a mechanic. It wasn't that I thought a mechanic was a bad job, it just wasn't a very lucrative one, or one that would allow for much travel.

"Yeah, it's been my dream for a while now." He continued talking about the shop and I looked out the window. He stopped at the last stop sign before the turnoff to my house and asked, "Are you okay?"

I smiled. "Yeah, just imagining what it would be like to live in a small town where you were the mechanic."

"It sounds great, doesn't—"

The sound of metal being ripped open next to me interrupted him and made me jerk towards him in reaction. Hands covered in fur grabbed ahold of me, and yanked me towards the open door.

I grabbed onto Iagan's hands and screamed, "Let me go!"

Iagan gripped my hands and pulled me towards him, but the other person released the tension a moment and then yanked hard, jerking our hands apart. I scrambled with my hands, trying to find anything to grab onto while I kicked and tried to injure the person attempting to steal me. I saved myself from being pulled out of the car at the last second by grabbing onto the inside of the door jamb.

Iagan got out of the car and shifted into battle form. I looked back and found a wolf in battle form pulling on me. Two more wolves came out of the forest and attacked Iagan. I released my grip and shifted into my battle form. The wolf who had been trying to pull me out of the car swiped at me with large claws, narrowly missing my face. I hissed and swung back at him, scratching his arm. I roared as loudly as I could, calling for Dad's help.

I lunged forward and attacked the wolf, pushing him back towards the forest and closer to my pride. I had to hope that Iagan either defeated the two wolves that he was fighting with or that we could keep them at bay until my pride came. I glanced at Iagan and was shocked to find him cut up, bleeding, and moving slowly. The two wolves that were fighting him had a couple of cuts, but Iagan was definitely the worse for wear. I kicked the wolf I was fighting in the head and ran over to him, drawing the attention of one of the wolves away and hoping to give him some help.

"Grab her!" the wolf I had been fighting yelled. "Before her pride gets here!"

I sunk my claws into the lower chest of the wolf I was now fighting and jerked down, tearing through flesh and muscle and revealing rib bones. The wolf swung at me wildly in pain, and I darted backwards, right into the arms of a new wolf who had arrived as backup with six others. Why were there so many wolves?

Iagan screamed my name and roared at the wolves. My dad roared from the tree line and I turned, watching him and the rest of my pride race forward and start fighting the wolves.

"Retreat!" the wolves yelled. I smiled, thinking we had won, but the smile quickly left my face as the wolf holding me started trying to carry me away.

I kicked and squirmed, trying to get free and trying to find flesh to bite into. The wolf had me in a perfect hold though, and I could not get free. I started shifting into my animal form, hoping to get free and attack them, but the wolf grabbed a hold of my throat and cut off my air, forcing me to stop shifting and stop using excess energy. "Not today, little girl."

"Ainsley!" Dad roared from somewhere behind us.

What was happening? Why were the wolves attacking all of a

sudden? And why take me? I struggled more and the wolf squeezed harder until I passed out from lack of oxygen.

I WOKE UP WITH A MASSIVE HEADACHE AND SORE ARMS. I MOVED MY arms, trying to lift my torso up off of the ground, but I felt incredibly woozy and could barely open my eyes. What was wrong with me? What had they done?

"Keep her drugged so she can't change!" someone snapped nearby me. "Alpha will be here soon and then he will decide how to kill her."

Kill me? No. No. I am not going to die here. I haven't even left the state yet! I'm too young to die!

I forced my eyes open and my hopes dwindled at the sight of at least twenty werewolves standing around me. It looked like we were in some type of empty warehouse. I could smell dust and rats and rat droppings so it must be an abandoned warehouse.

Where was Dad? Where was Iagan? Didn't anyone follow the wolves as they took me away?

Someone grabbed my arm and then something pierced my skin. "Ow," I said softly despite my attempt to yell it. I really did not like these drugs. They sucked.

Warm liquid was pushed into me, and my eyes closed again. *This sucks.*

I fought to stay conscious, but was unsuccessful.

The dream started off like most of mine usually did, with me running through a forest chasing an animal, but then the scenery shifted. I was standing in front of a mirror, but instead of seeing my reflection I was looking at a reflection of Ethan.

"Where are you?" he asked me.

"Huh?" I asked intelligently.

"Where are you?" he asked again.

"Dreaming," I answered. "I think." He looked really good without his shirt on. Wait, when had he taken his shirt off?

"Focus, Ainsley. Where are you?" he asked as he stepped closer to the mirror.

"Warehouse," I whispered as I reached out towards him. "On the floor."

"Show me," he whispered.

"Drugs," I said as I looked at the scar on his chest. The scar was a crescent shape on the right side of his chest. How had he gotten that? Who had hurt him?

He pressed his hand against the mirror and whispered, "I will come save you."

I reached out to press my hand against the mirror to touch his, but the scenery shifted again, putting me back in the warehouse with the wolves surrounding me. "No more," I whispered, "No more drugs." I reached out for Ethan who was standing in the middle of the wolves, but I could not pick my body up. "Ethan," I whispered. "Run."

A wolf hit me in the face and the dream faded away. I wanted to help Ethan, but when my eyes opened, I realized that I was the one who needed to be saved, not him. A new wolf who had a very large scar through his eye stared down at me and he did not look happy to see me.

"What?" I asked as the fogginess began to clear and feeling returned to my body.

He dropped me and I could not save my head from hitting the ground. It hurt and I whined in pain. Why was my heart beating so slowly?

"You gave her too much," he growled at one of the other wolves. "You could have killed her."

"Aren't we going to kill her anyways?" the wolf asked.

The new wolf slapped him so hard that he flew backwards, sliding across the warehouse floor. I wiggled my fingers and toes, trying to get movement back through my limbs now that I had feeling.

"We are going to kill her when and how I want. Now is not the time for her to die," the new wolf said. He walked back over to me and sat me up, leaning me against the wall so he could look at me. I tried to support myself, but it took most of my strength just to keep my head upright. "Where is he? Where is the other super lion?"

"What?" I asked. "There's no super lion." He must have taken some of the drugs they'd been giving me.

The wolf slapped me across the face and that was when I felt his aura. He was an alpha werewolf and judging by the amount of fear I felt within me, he was a very strong alpha. "Where is the lion you have been dating? Where is the other lion like you?"

"I don't know," I whispered honestly. "I don't know where they are."

"They?" he asked and then laughed. "I am not talking about that pathetic lion we stole you from. I am talking about the Ra or Ro or whatever you call him. The one who is stronger than other lions. The one who did this!" he yelled at the end, pointing to his face. "Where is he?"

"I don't know," I said again. "Today was not his day with me."

"It's not today, it's already the next day," he said. "What is his name? What is he under in your contacts on your phone?"

Should I tell him? What would happen if I did? Would Ethan really come? He would be killed if he came here. There were too many wolves for one lion to take on. Maybe he could call my dad and the entire pride would come to get me. Did I want that? Or would the wolves kill them all?

"No," I said as I rotated my ankles, finally getting mobility back in them.

"No?" the alpha asked. "Did you really just tell me, no?"

"I won't let you bring him here just to kill him," I said.

"You don't have a choice," he snarled. "Either you tell me his name or I kill you and string your dead body up by your entrails with a note of where to find me so that he and I can finish our battle. Either you die now or I kill you once I defeat him and make him watch. I would prefer the latter, but I like either one."

I swallowed nervously. I did not want to die, but I did not want to watch Ethan die either. "You're going to kill me no matter what. I would rather die alone, than watch you hurt him and then die."

"You do not have a choice. You will tell me his name," he said as he stood up. "Mark and Antoine, hold her. James take a video on her cell phone. I'll beat the name out of her or I will just send everyone in her contacts the video."

"No!" I screamed as I scrambled away from the wall and tried to run. I stumbled and tripped my way across the warehouse, but I could not shift with the drugs still in my system. Two of the wolves grabbed me and pulled my arms behind my back. "Let go!" I screamed. "Let go of me!"

The alpha walked towards me with another wolf holding my cell phone up and videotaping. "Scream all you want, no one will hear you."

I struggled against them, trying to free myself, but the drugs still had me weakened and there were two holding me. The alpha slapped me across the face again, so hard that my head whipped to the side. I snarled at him, showing him my teeth. He punched me in the stomach, making my breath rush out of me.

I inhaled deeply and then growled at him again. "Screw you," I whispered.

He changed his hand into a wolf's paw and showed me his claws. "I have no qualms about tearing you apart and using your bits to make a trail."

"My pride will come here and my alpha will rip your head off," I whispered. "You will only be leaving a trail to your demise."

"Who is the Ra? What is his name!" he screamed.

"Bite me," I said with a smile.

"Fine," he whispered. He turned away from me and then spun around with his hand in an arc, slicing his claws through my chest and reopening my old scar.

I screamed in pain and jerked one of my hands free from the wolf holding me. He tried to grab me again, and I punched him in the face. I stomped on the wolf still holding me, catching the instep of his foot, and making him release his grip. I ran and stumbled away, using the adrenaline in my body to fuel my escape. I made it to the door, and then the alpha jumped onto my back in his wolf form, digging his claws into my shoulders and legs to keep me down and then bit my arm. I screamed in pain and tried my hardest to get away.

The alpha bit down harder, his teeth grazing my bone and making me scream even louder. I wanted to change. I needed to change. I could win if I changed. The alpha switched forms again and said, "Send the video to all of the male names in her phone."

"No!" I screamed.

"Drugs," the alpha commanded.

A wolf came and jabbed a needle into my arm, injecting me with the awful drugs again. I needed to stay awake to treat my wounds, but the drugs were too strong. I growled angrily and then succumbed to the weight of my eyelids.

I WOKE AGAIN AND HAD A NOW FAMILIAR SENSE OF WEAKNESS. I opened my eyelids slowly and was shocked to be in an upright position. I turned my head and found my arms tied to the walls. At least I was no longer lying in rat urine and feces. Unfortunately, I was now completely vulnerable and incapable of protecting myself, which was not an improvement.

"Check on the patrols, they should have been back by now," the alpha growled.

"They're probably dead," I whispered as I began the process of flexing my hands and feet to return the feeling to my limbs again. I really hated doing the same thing more than once.

"Shut up," he said. "Or I will drug you again."

Something crashed loudly outside and four of the wolves ran to investigate. I prayed it was my pride. I needed it to be them. I knew the alpha wolf would not let me live much longer, especially because of my big mouth.

"I hope you brought enough wolves with you. It takes a lot of wolves to take down a single lion. I really don't think you'll be able to defeat a pride of lions with a pack of wolves."

"Gag her," the alpha commanded. "Before I slit her throat."

"You say the nicest things," I whispered as I rolled my head around on my neck. "I bet your mate feels so lucky to have you."

The wolf who had videotaped the alpha beating me put a piece of cloth into my mouth and tied it around behind my head. "Be quiet, girl, before he decides to kill you early."

"No one will be killing her," Ethan said in a much deeper voice than normal. I turned my head towards the sound of his voice and saw him and Iagan in their battle forms, walking into the warehouse. Wolves ran at them and Ethan and Iagan quickly sliced them open with their claws.

I tried to say something, but the damn rag in my mouth prevented me from being able to. The alpha shifted into his battle form and walked towards me. "We will end this now."

I struggled against my binds, but of course it was no use.

The alpha wrapped his paw around my throat, pressing his claws again my skin. "If you want her to live, stop immediately."

Ethan and Iagan dropped the wolves they had been about to throw at other wolves and growled.

Iagan said, "Drop her now."

"The Ra and I have unfinished business. I challenge you."

"You lost then and you will surely lose now," Ethan growled. "Let the female go and I will fight you."

"You will fight me and when I win, I will kill her right in front of you," the alpha growled.

"You cannot accept his challenge," Iagan hissed. "We can defeat all of the wolves here and save her."

"If you attack his wolves, he will slit her throat and she will be dead!" Ethan yelled. "What good will it do to kill the wolves if she is dead, you idiot?"

"If—" Iagan began but Ethan hissed at him.

"Shut up. Let the adults handle this," Ethan said. Iagan growled, but stayed where he was as Ethan walked towards the alpha and me. "I accept your challenge."

I jerked against the binds and the alpha and screamed at him not to, but he ignored me.

"I'm glad someone here is smart," the alpha sneered. "Warrior forms only."

Ethan nodded his head. "Fine." He looked at me and smiled. "I told you I will always find you."

"If that cub so much as moves, kill the girl," the alpha ordered.

Ethan looked at Iagan and said, "Do not do something stupid. Stay there and let me handle this."

The alpha ordered two of his wolves to guard me and then walked to the center of the warehouse. There were still at least fifteen wolves inside the warehouse and Iagan was surrounded.

Where was my dad? Where was my pride? I wanted to change forms, but even if I did and I escaped from the binds holding me to the wall, the wolves guarding me would just attack me and kill me. What could I do? Could I help Ethan?

The alpha and Ethan squared off in the center of the warehouse and Ethan smiled. "I have been looking forward to giving you a matching scar on your other eye for quite some time."

"I will rip your heart out of your chest," the alpha growled.

Their fight began, and then all hell broke loose as my pride ran into the warehouse and started attacking the wolves. The two wolves guarding me looked at each other in confusion. The alpha had ordered them to kill me if Iagan did something, not if other lions came in. The alpha was too busy with Ethan to be able to give orders, so the wolves guarding me decided on their own and ran into the fray, attacking my dad and Lucy.

I shifted forms and my increased mass broke the binds and freed me. I jumped into the fight, attacking a wolf that was attempting to attack Stacy. She winked at me in her battle form and we stood back to back, fighting with the wolves.

Dad rushed over to me and asked, "Are you hurt?"

"A little, but I should heal by tomorrow," I assured him.

"Who is the alpha?" he asked, his fur bristling with anger.

"The one fighting with Ethan. He challenged Ethan."

Dad growled. "Then I cannot help him until the fight is over."

I wanted to help Ethan, but I knew I would only get in the way. I leaned against my dad, feeling extremely tired and despite wanting to keep my pride, I was too weak and needed assistance to stand. I looked around and was pleased to see that we had defeated all of the other wolves. All that was left was for Ethan to kill the alpha.

Dad wrapped an arm around my waist and lifted, holding me upright. Iagan walked over to me and asked, "Are you alright?"

I nodded. "Yes."

The alpha yelled in pain and we all turned towards them. Ethan had sliced open his other eye. "I told you that you would not win," Ethan said. "Now I will kill you."

He grabbed the alpha who was too slow from being weakened and snapped his neck. Ethan let the body fall to the ground and then roared in triumph. He turned around, searching for me and when our eyes locked, he gave me his best cocky smirk. I smiled back at him and then passed out.

CHAPTER NINE

"Ainsley, it's time to wake up," Dad said from near me. "You have slept long enough."

I opened my eyes and looked at his face over mine. "Hi."

He smiled. "Hello."

"What happened after I blacked out?" I asked as I sat up.

Dad sat down on the end of my bed. "I carried you home and laid you on your bed and you have been here for four hours."

"Are Ethan and Iagan alright?" I asked. I felt more concerned for the first than the second. I knew I had already made my decision, especially because of the way both had handled my kidnapping and rescue, but I was not willing to admit that to anyone yet. Plus, I still had some very important questions to ask Ethan before I would announce anything.

"Yes," he said. "Both have been waiting to see how you are."

I stood up and groaned because my muscles were still sore. "Apparently four hours was not enough time for my muscles to fully recuperate."

"You'll be fine as soon as you eat," he said as he pet the top of my head. "You should go speak to the males before they pace a hole in my floor." He looked at my clothes and said, "Maybe you should shower and change first though."

I could smell the rat urine and feces in my hair still so I already knew that. "Will you tell them that I am alright and I will meet them as soon as I am done?"

He nodded and walked out of my room. I grabbed fresh clothes and limped my way to the bathroom. The hot water felt amazing on my sore body and even though I had some of the best shampoo and soap, I washed myself three times thoroughly before getting out of the shower and getting dressed. I brushed my teeth and stared at my reflection as I replayed all of the recent events. How had Ethan and Iagan found me? Had the wolves sent them an address? And what was up with the dream I had had with Ethan? Was it just a dream? I knew there were some lions who could communicate even in the dream world, but I had not met anyone yet who could do it with me. Was it because of the Ra and Sekhmet thing?

Oh my god! I had to do my project still. What was today?

I ran out of the bathroom and towards the living room. "What day is today?"

"Sunday," Ethan said as he walked out of the living room and into the hallway.

Sunday. "How can it be Sunday? What happened to Saturday?" I asked. How had I missed it?

"The wolves had you for an entire day," Iagan said as he stepped into the hallway.

Wow. That could explain why I had been having trouble shifting. The drugs and the lack of nutrition would have severely inhibited me. "I have a project due tomorrow and I have not even started on it," I said as I tried to absorb the fact that I had lost an entire day.

"I can help you," Ethan said.

"No, you can't. Today is not your day," Iagan said angrily.

"No fighting," I said before Ethan could say the violent

thought that was very obviously on his mind. "I will do the project myself, but that means you two need to leave." I felt awful about kicking them out, but I really had to do the project. I hoped I would be able to finish it in time for school tomorrow. "Thank you both for coming to rescue me," I said seriously, trying to keep from looking at Ethan more than Iagan since Iagan had been more of a hindrance than anything. "I appreciate you both working together to save me."

"I would do anything for you," Ethan whispered as he walked closer to me.

Iagan grabbed his arm and pulled him back. "Of course we worked together. We both wanted to save you."

"Hands off," Ethan growled.

"Time to go, boys," Dad said as he walked into the hallway.

"Thank you again, both of you," I said with a smile at them both. "I will see you tomorrow Ethan and Iagan I will see you Tuesday."

They both smiled and then Iagan glared at Ethan as he walked in front of him to leave. Ethan winked at me and then followed Iagan out of the house.

Dad sighed and ran a hand through his hair. "Those boys are a handful."

"Yep," I said as I headed back towards my room. "I'm going to grab my laptop and then I will eat in the kitchen while I work."

"I'll make you some food," Dad said. "By the way, your mom called, worried about you. She asked that you call her as soon as you are available."

"Okay," I said softly. I wasn't sure if I really wanted to talk to her right now. I still felt hurt that she had left me, even though I knew she was probably much happier now. Should I call her? I pushed it out of my mind for now, focusing on grabbing my stuff and working on my project.

It took me three hours to finish it, but I had made a perfect project. I was as proud of it as I would have been if it had been a project that I had worked on all weekend. I ate again and then soaked in a hot bath. I closed my eyes and tried to let all of the previous day's events drain away from me. I sighed in relaxation and slid farther down in the tub until the water was just below my chin. If I could do this every day, I would be a lot less angry all of the time.

"I need to shower," Lucy called through the door.

"Alright," I groaned as I stood from the tub and pulled the plug to let the water drain. I dried off and headed to my room, getting dressed in my pajamas and then flopping down on my bed.

"Are they the ones you have been ignoring me for?" a familiar voice asked from behind me.

I spun around and stared in shock at Felix. "How did you get in here? What are you doing here?" I climbed off of the bed and started backing towards my door. He was only human, but I still did not like him being in here with me. "Dad!" I called.

"Are they the ones you are interested in? Is it because of their weird smells? Is that why you like them?" he asked, walking towards me with strangely amber eyes.

"What happened to you?" I asked him. I inhaled and my eyes widened in shock. He smelled like a wolf.

"A guy came to me and asked if I wanted to be stronger. He asked if I wanted to improve my life and be wanted by girls," he said as he moved closer to me.

I continued backing up and hit my back against my door. I reached for the door handle and heard my dad coming down the hallway.

"He changed into a wolf!" Felix said with a deranged laugh. "I had never expected that to be real, but he was a real live were-wolf. He bit me and now, now I am better." He stepped closer to me and whispered, "Now we can be together."

"No, we can't," I whispered and then jerked the door open and stepped into the hallway, bumping into dad.

"Who is that?" Dad asked.

"Why not?" Felix asked angrily. "What is it about them that is better than me?!"

"Is he a werewolf?" Dad asked as he inhaled his scent. "How did he get in here? What do you want?"

"I want her to admit why she is not interested in me!" Felix screamed.

"He was the human boy I was friends with," I told Dad. "He was bitten by some wolf and he came here."

"Leave the house now, or I will be forced to remove you," my dad said angrily. "Friend or not, you cannot be here."

"I'm a werewolf now. I'm stronger and faster and better than humans," Felix said.

"Exactly. You are a werewolf, but I am not," I said.

"What?" he asked. "I thought you were. He said you were like me."

I shook my head. "I'm not a wolf," I said. "I'm sorry, but you and I cannot be together."

"Tell me why!" he screamed, his eyes changing into wolf's eyes and his skin beginning to crawl.

"You are a wolf and she is a lion," Dad said. "Our kinds do not mix."

"Lion?" Felix asked. He laughed. "That's why they are your favorite animal. Theresa will laugh when she finds out."

"You can't tell Theresa," I said. "You can't be around her until you learn to control yourself. If you were to change at school you would..."

"Don't tell me what to do!" he screamed at me.

Dad pushed me behind him and shifted into battle form. "Leave before I force you to," Dad said again.

Felix looked at him with fear and asked, "How do you shift like that?"

Dad reached for him and Felix shifted into his wolf form out of fear and the need to protect himself.

"Felix, just calm down," I urged him. "It does not have to end this way."

He snarled and launched himself at me, claws extended and mouth opened in a snarl. Dad grabbed him by the throat and sunk his claws in, tearing holes into Felix's throat. I sobbed and turned my head away.

"Go to your room," Dad ordered. "I will take care of this."

I obeyed, not wanting to see Felix's dead body. Why had it come to this? Why did he have to come here? What was I going to say to Theresa?

As I walked into school, I fought with myself over what to say to Theresa or if I should say anything. Should I just lie and say I haven't heard from him? His parents would be filing a missing person's report soon, and I could not get my family involved in that. Dad had not spoken to me after he had sent me to my room, and his car was gone when I left for school. I really did not want to know what he did with Felix's body and I was glad not to have the opportunity to ask him. It gave me more of an alibi to not know what had happened. I knew what I needed to say to Theresa, but it made me feel like a bad guy.

"Ainsley," Chuck said in a strange voice. "Hi."

I turned around and his scent wafted to me. Werewolf. What the hell was going on? Who was turning these guys at my school?

"'Sup Chuck?" I said, trying to sound playful even though I was now incredibly nervous.

"You can sense the difference in me, can't you?" he asked as he walked towards me. "The other girls can, too, and they like the fear they feel and the knowledge that they are in the presence of someone dangerous."

"Who did this to you?" I asked him, trying to keep my distance from him without him realizing what I was doing. It would not be a good idea to upset a new werewolf at a school filled with humans.

"He offered me power and extreme strength. All of the pain and strange side effects are worth it. I am invincible!" he said loudly.

"No, you're not," I said in a flat tone. "Why are you at school? Do you think you are ready to be around humans? If you change in front of them you will damn us all." What was I going to do? I needed to figure out a way to get him away from school and to a pack that would deal with him and the rogue who was changing them. Wait. What if it wasn't a rogue and it was the pack that was doing it? Were they trying to kill me?

My cell phone vibrated and I pulled it out of my pocket, pleased to see a text from Ethan.

Ethan: *Hey, want to ditch school?"*

I quickly texted him back.

Me: *Meet me here now. Help.*

"Who are you texting?" Chuck asked. "Is it your boyfriend? Do you still think he is better than me? I am like you now. I did not understand before why you would not let me date you, but now I can see why you wanted to keep your distance from me. We've fixed that though. Now we are the same and we can be together."

This sounded very familiar. What was this wolf who was changing them telling them? Had he been watching us and knew that both Felix and Chuck had a thing for me? Was that why he chose them to change? To try to trick them into thinking that the only reason I would not date them was because they weren't paranormal?

"Yes, it was my boyfriend. I do not think he is better than you, Chuck. He is just different. Why don't you come with me and ditch school? We could talk," I offered.

"How is he different?" he asked angrily. I could see the change in his eyes and knew if I made him any angrier that he would shift. He was not stable enough yet.

"I am a lion and you are a wolf," Ethan said as he walked up behind me.

"What is that supposed to mean?" Chuck asked angrily. "Is that some type of analogy or something? Because I assure you that I can kick your ass."

"Come on, Chuck. Let's go talk. I promise I will explain everything once we are away from the school. I can't risk the humans hearing," I whispered. I was smiling and trying to play sweet and innocent, but Chuck was already angry and now he was glaring at Ethan.

"Wasn't this guy a human a few days ago?" Ethan asked me softly.

I nodded.

Chuck smirked, "Yeah, I was, but now I am *super*human."

"Ethan, maybe you should come back later. I think you are only making him angrier," I said, feeling stupid for even asking Ethan to have come. I could have handled Chuck on my own.

"I am not leaving you alone with a new werewolf," he said sternly.

"I can handle myself," I said back to him, turning around to face him since I knew he would protect me if Chuck tried anything while my back was turned.

"I would not be able to forgive myself if something happened to you and I could have prevented it," he whispered, reaching out to stroke my cheek.

"Don't touch her," Chuck growled.

I had to diffuse the situation now, before Chuck went wolf. I stepped back from Ethan and said, "Trust me, okay?"

He clenched his jaw, but walked backwards, heading towards his motorcycle. Why hadn't I heard him ride up on it when I was talking to Chuck? "I will stay nearby. You call me, and I will be here."

"Thank you," I mouthed and then turned around and smiled at Chuck. "So, now that he is leaving, do you want to ditch with me? We can get food and go talk completely alone."

Chuck smiled wide and I knew that I had finally broken through. The idiot probably thought that I was rejecting Ethan for him. Poor idiot. "Sure, alright. Let's go."

"I'll drive," I said cheerily.

"*I hope that you know what you are doing.*" Ethan said telepathically from wherever he had driven to. Once a strong bond has been created, werelions could communicate telepathically over a ten-mile radius. Don't ask me why it was only ten miles, but that was what it was. Dad and I tested it.

I drove ten minutes away to the large open field with tall grass that most kids who ditched went to. The grass was tall enough that when you were sitting down, no one could see you from the street. I hoped it would be enough distance from the humans to be able to take Chuck down if I needed to.

"*I have everything under control. Besides, I can scream for help and I don't even need to open my mouth to let him know what I am doing.*"

"*If he hurts you I will kill him.*"

I smiled. "*You say the nicest things to me.*"

"What are you smiling about?" Chuck asked pleasantly as he sat down in the center of the field.

I sat down across from him, and we squashed the grass down between us so that we could see each other. "I was just thinking that we have not done this in a long time and that it's nice to get away from the school and all of the drama there."

He smiled back. "Yeah, it is nice to get away from it from time to time."

"So, why don't you tell me about the guy who changed you?" I asked nicely.

He shrugged. "He came to the school and offered me all the stuff I told you. I said I wanted it and so I followed him to the back field." He shivered and continued, "Then his face changed into this grotesque mixture of man and wolf and he bit me. It hurt like hell and I passed out from the pain."

"What did he look like?" I asked.

Chuck shrugged. "Male in his early thirties with brown hair and brown eyes. Six feet three inches tall and super ripped with a scar across his forehead."

My eyes widened as I recalled the face. It was the wolf that had attacked me, the one that Iagan had saved me from. It had to be. "What happened after that?" I asked him, trying to squash my fear down so I would not excite Chuck.

"I woke up and then shifted and he told me that now you and I were the same and that I should go find you as soon as possible. Unfortunately, I did not know where you lived so I just stayed home for the weekend and slept, looking forward to being able to see you today." He smiled and moved closer to me. "I have always thought that you were the most beautiful girl at school."

I smiled back and said, "Thank you, Chuck. I think you're great, but—"

"But what?" he asked angrily. "But you're with that tool? Isn't he a little old for you? What is he twenty?"

"When you change you are a wolf, right?" I said, trying to change the subject a little and keep him from getting angry.

"Yes," he said nodding. "Just like you."

I shook my head. "No, not like me. When I change forms I turn into a saber-toothed Smilodon, or lion as we call ourselves. You are a werewolf and I am a werelion."

"What do you mean a sabre-toothed smelly whatever?" he asked.

I sighed and shifted just my head into animal form, let him really get a look at it, and then shifted back. I shook my head because I hated how it felt to only change one part of my body. "See?" I said softly. "We are not the same. Wolves and lions do not get along. We are rival predators and cannot interbreed."

Chuck sat in silence for a while as he absorbed what I had said. "Can I switch animals?" he asked.

I shook my head. "No, once you are infected with the disease, that is the only one you can have. If I bit you it would just hurt a lot."

"He lied to me," he whispered angrily. He stood up and screamed, "He lied to me!"

I stood up and reached out, setting my hand on his arm. "It's alright, we—"

He swatted my hand away and spun around, teeth bared. "You ruined my life! I did this so we could be together and now you want to take that lion over me!"

"You ruined your own life by trying to become something that you are not. That wolf ruined your life by biting you. I did not do anything," I said, standing my ground.

His body started shaking, and I slapped him across the face, distracting him from the change. "Knock it off. Now is not the time to shift. Do you want to kill innocent humans just because you were stupid and let some guy bite you?"

He growled at me and in a split second he changed forms. He growled at me again and I sighed. So much for handling the problem. *"He shifted."*

"I see that."

I did not turn around because I did not want to expose my back to Chuck. "Chuck, just calm down."

He growled at me and swiped his paw towards me. I put my hands on my hips and glared at him. "Don't think that I won't fight you. If you want me to, I will."

"You will do no such thing," Ethan said as he walked up behind me. "You will go to your car and leave so that Chuck and I can have a little chat."

"No way. I am not letting you kill him. It is not his fault…"

"I'm not going to kill him," Ethan said, interrupting me. "You being here is only going to exacerbate matters. Now go to the car and drive back to school. I will talk with him, and he will leave perfectly alive and well." I stared at him, not sure if I believed him. "I promise," he said.

I did not want to leave, but I could not see any way to help the current situation. "Fine," I said, "But you better text me after."

"I'll do better than that. I will tell you exactly what happened. Deal?" He said with a smirk as he faced Chuck who was just watching us.

"Deal." I walked away, hoping that Chuck did not escalate things until the point that Ethan would have to hurt him. Why was the wolf doing this? Did he want the world to find out about werewolves and the existence of all paranormals?

I could understand not wanting to be the one who came out about it, because then you would be the one that scientists wanted to experiment on. If he turned some random kid into a wolf he would not care if the scientists tore him apart with their experiments and he would still expose the werewolves to the world. Why do it, though? It would most likely start a witch hunt that would tear families and friends apart as they tried to find others.

I drove to school and then sat in my car as I tried to figure out what the point of all of the things that had happened to me were. Nothing really came to mind so I went into the school and made my way to the cafeteria since it was lunch time, and I was hungry.

"Hey, where have you been?" Theresa asked as she got into line beside me.

"Sorry, I was having an argument with someone," I half lied. "What's up?"

"I finally got the courage and went over to Felix's house," she said and then shivered. She leaned closer and whispered, "Both of his parents were dead and he was nowhere to be found. I called the cops and had to deal with them and explain why I was there. It was a huge fiasco."

"His parents are dead?" I asked softly. I didn't think my dad would have killed them. There was no way to connect Felix to us, but if my dad had felt they would threaten the pride then he might have. I swallowed nervously, really hoping that he had not done it.

"Yeah, they looked like they were attacked by some type of animal," she whispered. "It was nasty."

Oh no.

"You okay? You turned all pale," she asked and set her hand on my forearm.

I smiled, trying my best to hide my true feelings. "Sorry, I just let my imagination run away with itself and pictured it. I'm so sorry that you had to see that. Are you okay?" I asked, trying to play her friend even though the only thing I really wanted to do was leave and go home.

"Yeah, I'm alright. I've seen some pretty gross stuff before so it didn't faze me too much," she said with a straight faced lie.

Good for her. I liked a girl that didn't run around screaming and crying.

"He is sound asleep in his bed at his house," Ethan said to me.

"Thank you. Did he cause you too much trouble?"

"You owe me a back massage."

I laughed and Theresa looked at me like I was crazy. "Um, sorry I just got a joke that my dad had told me this morning."

"Maybe that can be part of our date tonight," I tempted him.

"You're on."

"Have you heard from Felix at all?" Theresa asked. "It's just so weird that he would disappear like that."

I shook my head. "He hasn't called me." That was true, he had shown up at my house. "I wonder if whatever killed his parents took him."

Theresa shuddered. "If they did, I don't think he'll be found alive."

I patted her back. "I'm sorry."

"Death is common around me," she whispered. "It's like I'm a curse."

No, I was the curse, but I could not tell her that. "It has nothing to do with you and you know it. Do not blame yourself."

We grabbed food and headed back towards our spot, both stewing in silence as we thought about Felix. Could it have been the wolf after me that killed Felix's parents? Was he going to try to set up my pride for their murders since Felix had come to our house? I took my cell phone out and excused myself to call my dad.

I walked to the bus turnaround where it was currently void of any humans and dialed my dad. "Yes, Ainsley."

"You remember when I was younger and a wolf attacked me and gave me the scar on my chest?"

"Yes," he said questioningly.

"I think he is back to get me again."

"Are you in danger?" he asked. "Do I need to come get you?"

"Not at the moment," I said. I looked around to ensure no one was nearby and whispered, "Felix's parents are dead."

"Who's Felix?"

I sighed. "The wolf last night."

He was silent a moment and then said, "It wasn't me."

I exhaled in relief. "Okay."

"This could mean trouble for us," he said angrily. "If that jerk is trying to make it seem like we did it—"

"There's more I have to tell you, but obviously it needs to wait until I get home," I said, "I need to go though."

"Where's Ethan?" he asked.

"Hold on, let me see if he is still in range and I will ask him." *"Ethan?"*

"Yes?"

"Where are you?"

"Eating. You need me?"

"He's eating."

"Ask him to come see me," Dad said. "Get back to school and then hurry home afterwards. Keep your eyes and ears open and protect yourself."

"My alpha wants to see you as soon as possible."

"Okay. I'm heading there now."

I put my phone away and headed back towards Theresa who was playing with her cell phone and eating fries from her tray of food.

"Sorry about that," I said, "My mom and dad split up this weekend."

"I'm sorry. My parents split up, too. It will get easier."

"Who left who?" I asked, curious how she had handled matters.

"My dad left us. Just bounced to Mexico."

"Did you talk to him after that?" I asked.

She nodded. "I did, but not for like three years. I was so mad that I could not handle talking to him."

I sighed. "I haven't talked to my mom since she left. I feel abandoned, almost, even though my dad is taking care of me."

"I just had to remind myself that he did not leave me, but left my mom. It was not about me and not that he did not love me anymore, it was the fact that he and my mom did not get along," she said.

I nodded, understanding. "Yeah, you're right."

"You could text her and then you would not have to talk to her right away," she suggested.

I smiled. "That is a great idea," I said sincerely.

"I have them occasionally."

We laughed and then the bell rang, signaling the end of the lunch. "Does it seem like lunch keeps getting shorter and shorter?" I asked her as we stood up.

She nodded. "I was just thinking that."

"So, how is it going with the boy problems?" she asked me with a smirk.

"Well, I think I have decided on one, but I don't want to jinx myself yet. I still have to ask him a few things before I decide."

She laughed. "Dang you are acting like you're marrying him. It's just a boyfriend."

I shook my head. "I told you it's more of an arranged marriage thing. Once I pick a guy I am stuck with him for life."

"*Stuck?*" Ethan asked. "*Is that how you really feel?*"

"*How did you hear that?*" I asked nervously. Could he hear everything that I said?

"*You and I have a unique connection, Ainsley. I am aware of a lot more than you know. Don't avoid my question. Do you feel that you would be stuck with me?*"

"*I will discuss it with you tonight.*"

I ignored anything else he might have tried to say and put my headphones in, pulling up the hood of my sweatshirt to hide them from the teacher. I made it through the last class with no problems and then hurried home, parking and staring at the police car in the driveway with fear.

I looked up at the house and saw dad talking to a police officer. Oh no. What had happened? I got out of the car and walked slowly up to the porch. "What's going on?" I asked.

The officer turned around and smiled at me. He was a large man, close to six feet tall with arms as big as my dad's. If he had been a lion, I would have been very nervous about him being on our land. "Hello. You must be Ainsley."

I nodded. "Yes."

"I just have a few questions to ask you. You're not in trouble or anything, sweetheart. We're just looking for a missing boy."

"Felix," I offered.

He nodded. "So, you know he is missing?"

"My friend Theresa told me today. She told me last week that he was really sick and he missed a few days of school and then she came to school today and told me that he was missing."

"Is that all she told you?" he asked, giving me his cop stare.

"No, she also told me that Felix's parents were dead," I admitted. "Who would kill his parents? Do you know if Felix is still alive?" I asked, feigning concern.

The cop wrote down a couple of things in his notebook and shook his head. "We are still looking into it. I wouldn't worry about your friend though. None of the blood found at the scene was his."

"You don't think he could have done it, do you?" I asked, letting the color drain from my face.

The cop shook his head. "It was a wolf that had gotten loose from the zoo. We captured it and put it down."

"How awful," I whispered, seriously horrified that an innocent wolf had just been killed because of the man after me.

"Thank you for talking with me. You all have a good day."

I walked up to dad and we watched as the officer walked to his car and drove away. "Was that okay?" I asked my dad.

He nodded. "You did great."

I exhaled and rubbed my face. "This is so crazy. Did Ethan come here?"

He nodded again and then opened the front door and waited for me to step inside. "He did. He said he had to run an errand real quick, and then he would be back for your date."

I walked to my dad's study and sat down in one of the chairs. "Did he tell you everything?"

Dad nodded. "I'm hoping that the stupid wolf tries something here so I can rip his head off."

I flipped my phone around in my hand and asked, "What do you think about Ethan and Iagan?"

Dad smiled at me. "What do you think of them?"

"Dad," I groaned. "Just answer my question."

He laughed. "They're both decent lions as far as I have seen. Ethan is more dominant and is a Ra, which is better for your bloodlines, but Iagan being less dominant than you would make you being in charge easier."

"I don't want to be in charge," I said.

"Ethan has proven that he can protect you, and I was not impressed with Iagan especially since he let the wolves take you."

Neither was I. "Yeah, that incident really pushed Ethan into the front runner's spot."

"Iagan did protect you when you were younger, but I think that now, you have surpassed him and you would need to protect him more than he would you."

I sighed. "Those are my exact thoughts."

He smiled at me. "I know. Just remember that you are Sekhmet. You could choose both of them. Iagan may end up becoming stronger, especially if you take Ethan as a mate. But, whoever you choose, you will be with them the rest of your life. Your mother and I had a different arrangement in which I allowed her to leave. You may not be so lucky."

"I know."

"Whoever you choose will be the lucky one," Dad said. "And you know that as long as you are happy, I will be happy, too."

"I better go change," I said as I stood up. "Thank you."

"Anytime."

I walked into my room and shut my bedroom door. I was pretty sure I was going to choose Ethan, but I still needed to talk to him about the mates thing.

Fur covered hands wrapped around my mouth and waist and pulled me backwards against a furry body. "Hello, darling."

I tried to scream, but his hand was covering my mouth.

"No screaming. We don't need to bring daddy in here."

"Dad!" I screamed telepathically. *"He's here!"*

My bedroom door flung open, falling off of the hinges from the force he had used to open it. "Back off," Dad growled.

"How did you—" the wolf asked.

"Let her go, and I will kill you quickly," Dad said as he walked towards us.

The wolf pulled his hand away from my mouth and then

pressed a cold metal barrel to my head. "Come any closer and I will shoot her in the head."

Dad stopped moving and growled. "Why are you doing this?"

"She ruined my honor!" the wolf screamed. "I was defeated by two cubs and have not been able to join a pack or take a mate because of it. I will kill her and that boy, and restore my honor."

I had no idea that wolves held grudges, but both of the wolves that had attacked me recently were because of past fights. "Killing me won't restore your honor. Neither will turning boys at my school into wolves."

"Oh, they aren't for restoring my honor. They are for outing the werewolves to the human race."

"Why?" my dad asked. "That would only start the witch hunts all over again."

"Precisely. While the humans run around killing each other, we will move away from them and watch them burn. Once they have crippled themselves, then we will step in and take our place."

"They will never accept you," I said with a shake of my head. "Humans cannot accept things more powerful than they are."

"You are young and naïve. Once they learn about our healing properties and the fact that we do not get sick and do not get cancer, they will line up to be bitten. Just look at the two boys who were willing to be turned for a chance to get more girls."

Sadly, it made a little bit of sense to me.

"You won't get away with this," Dad said. "There are groups to protect against such things."

The wolf laughed. "You really think they will come after me? I highly doubt it."

I was completely lost now. Who were they talking about? What was this group they mentioned?

I wanted to stomp on his foot, but I was afraid that he would squeeze the trigger and shoot me either on purpose or accident if

I did that. "Killing me still won't restore your honor," I said, "Especially if you kill me by using a human gun."

He stopped moving, and I knew he realized that I was right. "It won't matter how you die because no one will know anything except that you died."

"What's wrong? Why are you frightened?" Ethan asked.

I heard his motorcycle approaching and hoped he would stay away until we resolved this. I did not want him getting shot. *"I'm having a bit of a problem. Just wait outside."*

The wolf tightened his grip around my waist and then leapt through the window, taking me with him. I tried to get free of him now that the gun was not at my head, but he was very strong and I could not get out. I changed my head into a lion's and my hands into paws and scratched at him and then bit into his arm.

He yelled out in pain and then punched me in the face. I stumbled away from him, dodging behind a tree just as he pulled the trigger on the gun.

"Come back here and die properly," he shouted.

I shifted into battle form and ran from tree to tree, narrowly avoiding the bullets as he shot at me again and again. He ran forward and then I heard something hard hit him. I glanced around a tree and found Ethan sitting on the wolf's back and Dad standing next to him.

"Just wait outside, huh?" Ethan asked me.

Dad took the gun and using both hands bent the barrel at a ninety degree angle downwards, rendering it useless. "Only a pathetic paranormal uses a human weapon," he scolded.

"You think you've won, but I will hunt you down, girl. You will never be able to sleep soundly again. You will never—"

Ethan snapped his neck and said, "Now she will sleep like a baby." He stood up and looked at my dad. "I apologize if I overstepped boundaries."

Dad shook his head. "No, you are within your rights to kill him."

Ethan walked towards me, and I realized that I was still in my battle form and still hiding behind the tree. "He can't hurt you anymore," Ethan whispered.

"I told you that you hadn't won," the wolf said as he stood up and snapped his neck back into place.

Ethan and my dad ran forward, attacking the wolf who seemed as good as usual. I cowered behind the tree, recalling the night he had attacked me and the fear I had felt then.

"I am immortal," he called out to me. "I will find you wherever you go and kill you."

Dad grabbed him and snapped his neck again. "Ainsley start a fire. If we burn the body it will permanently kill him."

"Had a run in with an immortal before?" Ethan asked as he grabbed some branches from the ground.

Dad nodded. "Yes. They are usually too cocky for their own good, as you can see by him, and don't think most know how to kill them." Dad looked over at me and said, "Ainsley, start the fire."

I stared at the wolf's body, waiting for him to speak again. To come back to life again. I had killed him that night. I remembered now. I had stabbed a shard of glass through his heart and had thought I was safe. That was how he had hurt me. How do you kill something that won't die?

Ethan and Dad built a fire and as they were preparing to grab the wolf, he stood back up again. "I really hate that," he said as he rotated his neck around. "It is very painful, but no matter how many times you try, I will always get back up."

"No, you won't," Dad said and then changed his hand into a paw and slashed the wolf's throat.

The wolf laughed through his exposed throat, gurgling blood. I wanted to scream in terror at the sight, but then Ethan was in front of me, blocking my view. He grabbed my head and pushed it against his chest. "Don't watch."

I buried my face into his chest and inhaled his scent, trying to forget what I had just seen. I sat in Ethan's arms for ten minutes until my dad finally said, "It's over."

Ethan released me and stood. "Don't you think that it was odd that he was so easy to kill?" he asked Dad.

Dad shook his head. "I've seen it before. He was old and ready to die. He was just hoping to get revenge on Ainsley before we killed him, but ultimately his death was more important."

"How do you know?" I asked him. "How do you know he won't just stand up from the flames and—"

Ethan grabbed me and hugged me against him. "He's dead for good this time. You don't have to be scared anymore."

Before I could stop them, tears rolled out of my eyes and down my face. I sobbed and Ethan held me, whispering something to me, but I did not pay attention to the words. I cried until there were no more tears and then pulled away from him and wiped my face.

"Sorry," I mumbled and then had to clear my throat.

"It's alright."

"No, it's not," I said as I grew angry at myself. "I should have been able to stand up to him and I couldn't. I stood there like a pathetic little cub."

"Are you hurt?" Ethan asked.

I shook my head. "No."

"Are you hungry?" he asked.

I knew he was trying to change the subject and get my mind off of what had just happened, but how could I go anywhere if I was too afraid to protect myself in my own home?

"I'm not ready to be anyone's mate," I said as I backed away from him. "I can't be a mate to someone when I can't even stand up for myself."

"You are ready," Dad said. "Snap out of this."

I tensed, ready to run away, and Ethan grabbed me, sitting down and holding my back against his chest with my legs between his as we sat on the ground. "Relax. The big bad wolf is dead and everything is okay."

"Why would you still want me as a mate?" I asked him. "This is the second time you have had to rescue me."

"You are worth rescuing," he whispered into my ear as he rubbed my arms. "You are worth rescuing a million times over."

"You hardly know me," I whispered back.

"I know enough to want you as my mate," he whispered. "You are perfect."

"I'm a coward."

"All of us have moments of cowardice," he said. "Even me."

I could not believe that.

"It's true. One time I ran away from a fight."

"Why?" I asked. Why would someone as strong as Ethan run?

"Because at that time, I was not as strong as I am now. I was afraid that I would be killed so I ran away. You know what I learned?"

"What?" I asked, feeling my fear and embarrassment fading away.

"That to get over fear and the failure of running away, you must train harder and become a better lion."

"That's it?" I asked.

He nodded, his chin rubbing against the back of my head. "That's it."

I leaned my head back and exhaled. "I'm sorry."

He kissed my cheek. "Don't be. I like rescuing you."

"I'm hungry."

"Then let's go." He stood up and offered me his hand. I looked around and realized that my dad was gone. Where had he gone?

"Can we talk for a second?" I asked.

"Here?" he asked me. "Now?"

I nodded. "Yes."

He sat down and faced me. "Okay. What do you want to ask me?"

"Do you have any mates?"

He frowned. "I already told you that I do not have any. If you agreed to be my mate you would be my first."

Despite my wish to stay calm and rational, the recent situation only made my nervousness evident. We had talked about this before, but I needed his final answer. "What about after me? Are you going to acquire additional females? Are you just going to get a new female and forget all about me, only talking to me when you need to or when your other mates are mad at you?"

Like my dad had done with my mom.

He looked at my face a moment, trying to judge my emotions. "I would never forget about you."

"You avoided the main question," I said, scooting back from him.

He wrapped his hand around the base of my neck, pulling my face closer to his and said, "If I had you for a mate, I would not need any other mates. And, I would be understanding of you having additional mates."

"How do I know that you would keep your word on that? Would you seriously keep me as a mate or would you take me and then get another one once I had no option to search for someone else?" I asked.

His eyes changed into his lion's eyes and he spoke in a voice more lion than human. "If I make a promise, I keep it."

"If I choose you, would you make me the promise of only being with me?"

He moved his face closer to mine until his lips were a breath away from mine, his eyes staring into mine like fire. "I promise that if you agree to be my mate you will be my one and only mate until I die."

"Good answer," I whispered and then leaned forward, pressing my lips against his.

He wrapped me up in a giant hug, squeezing me against him. I purred against him and he purred back. "Does this mean what I think it means?" he asked. "Are you finally giving in and realizing that I am the best mate for you?"

"I know I was stubborn at first, but you proved to me that you are the best choice and I am happy that I have finally made my decision," I said with a smile as he continued to hold onto me.

"How many months until you turn eighteen?" he asked with a devilish smirk.

I nipped his chin and said, "Soon enough, Ethan."

He squeezed me and whispered, "I am very glad that you are mine."

We stood up, and I pulled out of his hold to admire his hotness. "Likewise."

"So, when do I get to tell the cub?" he asked.

I shook my head. "You are not telling anyone anything. I will tell you both who I choose tomorrow with my dad present in his office. That way I can try to keep you two from fighting."

"I don't need to fight him anymore. You already chose me," he said as he walked towards me.

I walked slowly away from him, heading in the direction of the river. "Maybe I should rescind my decision," I said with a smirk.

He took his shirt off, tossing it onto a nearby tree branch and asked, "Do you really want to give this up?"

"Conceited as always," I said with a shake of my head.

"You are going to have to get used to it. You will be with me for a very long time."

I ducked behind a tree and said, "If you can catch me."

I started to run away, but Ethan was already next to me and grabbed me in a bear hug. "You are not going anywhere. I do not want to chase after you again and rescue my damsel in distress."

"I'm not always a damsel in distress," I said angrily, feeling more embarrassed than anything.

He kissed my cheek and whispered, "I am only teasing you, Ainsley. Don't get mad."

It was hard to stay mad at him anyways. "I just hate that you have had to rescue me so many times."

"I know that you are very capable of taking care of yourself, but that's what mates are for. We are here to protect you and keep you safe," he whispered and then started petting my hair as he hugged me with one arm.

"So, where are we going on our trip?" I asked him.

"First, we will travel from California across the country to New York where we will fly to Rome," he said as he steered me back towards the house. "Then, we will travel north, visiting the important places in Italy along the way. Then, we will head west, taking a train to Paris."

"What about Switzerland?" I asked.

"We can make a detour if you would like to."

"How are we going to afford it?" I asked him. "Dad has some money saved for me, but it is really supposed to be used for a down payment on a house."

"You let me worry about the money," he said. "After our trip, we will figure out where to live and we will use your money as down payment if you would like. Okay?"

"You're not in the mob or something, are you?" I asked, tilting my head to the side so I could look up at him.

He laughed. "No."

"Are you going to elaborate on how you have money?" I asked, trying to get him to talk.

"I will explain everything after you have told Iago the news."

"Iagan," I corrected him.

"Parrot, cub, whatever. Neither will ever be able to defeat me. He might as well be a parrot."

"Be nice," I said. "You already won, so you don't need to make it worse by being overly cocky."

"Overly? Are you saying you don't think I could beat him?" he asked, pulling away from me.

I rolled my eyes. "Now you sound like him."

"That was mean."

I laughed and said, "You set yourself up for that one."

He grabbed my sides and started tickling me. "I'll show you a set up."

I screamed and tried to get away, but he was stronger than me. I leaned in and kissed him, distracting him and making his grip release and then ran away, hiding on the other side of my car.

"Ha!" I said victoriously.

"What's going on?" Iagan asked from the porch of the house.

We both turned and I stared at him in confusion. "It's not your night tonight."

"Your alpha told me the wolf I had rescued you from had returned. I came to see if you were okay," he said as he walked towards me, completely ignoring Ethan.

"Ethan and Dad killed him," I said.

"Dad?" Iagan asked.

"The alpha is her father," Ethan said as though he should have known that.

"Oh," he said. "So, are you really alright?" he asked, placing his hand on my upper arm.

Ethan growled. "Don't touch her."

"All three of you in my office, now," Dad called.

Iagan glared at Ethan. "Saved by her dad."

Iagan walked towards the porch, and I gave Ethan the look to chill out. He smirked at me and we walked to my dad's office. I stood between Ethan and Iagan and faced dad who was sitting in his chair. "Tell them," he said.

I turned around and looked at Ethan and then Iagan. "I have decided who I want as a mate."

"It hasn't been the two weeks yet," Iagan said, his brows furrowing. "Are you sure?"

I nodded and smiled. "I'm sure."

Iagan smiled and started to look smug.

"Iagan—" I began.

He yelled, "Ha! I knew it was—"

"I'm choosing Ethan," I said quickly.

His face went from elated to shocked to pissed off. "Are you serious? Why are you choosing him?"

"Because I can actually protect her and because I am a better match for her," Ethan said.

"She only started letting you court her because she wanted to protect her pride from being harmed by you," Iagan said angrily.

Ethan looked at me. "Is that true?"

I nodded. "Yes, but things changed once I spent time with you."

"You thought I would harm your pride? That I would really hurt them if you denied me?" Ethan asked angrily.

"I did not know you then. I only knew that you were a Ra and that because I was a Sekhmet that I had to let you court me," I tried to explain.

"So, you dated me because you had to?" he asked, growing angrier and angrier.

"That's probably why she chose you as well," Iagan said, enjoying the chaos he was creating.

"That's not true," I said as I faced Ethan. "I chose you because I want you to be my mate."

"Why?" he asked. "Why do you want me as a mate?"

It was too soon to admit that I loved him, but I was taking him as a mate so shouldn't I just tell him?

"Why are you just standing there?" he asked.

"You already know why I want you," I said angrily.

"To save her pride," Iagan taunted.

"Shut up!" Ethan and I yelled at him at the same time.

"If you had never come along, I would be her mate right now," Iagan said angrily.

"No, you would not have," I said. "You would have been killed by the wolves and then I would have been killed by them."

"Screw you. I can find a hundred females better than you," Iagan said bitterly. "I did not have to save you all those years ago, and I do not need a female who needs saving now!" He walked out of the office and left us alone.

Ethan shook his head at me and started to walk away. "I can't believe you thought I would hurt your pride."

"I'm sorry," I whispered.

He walked out of the office and slammed the door behind him. The click of the door sounded like it was an explosion inside of the room. It felt like a nail into my heart. Had I made the right decision? Would I regret this? Was Ethan coming back?

"He will be back," Dad said softly. "He just needs some time to cool off."

"Did I mess up?" I asked. "Was I wrong?"

"You chose wisely, and after he cools off, he will understand where you are coming from," he assured me.

I walked to my room and sat down on my bed.

Me: *I'm sorry. I know now that you would never have hurt me or my pride, but I did not know that for sure then. Please don't be mad at me. We should be celebrating.*

He did not respond to me, though. The silence inside of my head felt like a slap in the face. How was it my fault that I did not know him before? I knew him now and I knew now that he would not have hurt my pride. I changed into a nice dress and sat back down on my bed, holding my heels in my lap.

Me: *Whenever you want to go to dinner, I'm ready. I'll be waiting in my room.*

Still no response. I sent him a text message just to be sure that the reason he was not responding was not just because he was out of range.

Me: *I am sorry for hurting your feelings, but I did not know you then. I am dressed and waiting for you for dinner. I will wait for you in my room.*

I lay backwards on the bed and closed my eyes. Had things

been completely ruined? Was he going to leave now and find another mate? I waited for an hour and then started to fall asleep. I sat up and wiped the fresh tears from my eyes. Why was so much happening to me in such a short time? Couldn't I just have one ray of sunshine?

My cell phone vibrated and I opened it to read the text message.

Ethan: *Meet me at Caballo Blanco.*

Me: *On my way.*

I put my shoes on and headed out of the house, rushing to the restaurant and hoping that he had forgiven me. I walked to the hostess who smiled at me. "You must be Ainsley," she said.

I nodded. "Yes." How had she known?

"Right this way," she said and then led me towards the back of the restaurant. There were no other people in the restaurant despite it being the dinner rush time.

"Slow night?" I asked her.

"Sort of," she said. She stopped next to a set of double doors that led to a private room. "In here please."

I opened the doors and looked inside, sniffing before I entered to ensure that it was only Ethan there. He was sitting alone at a very long table with a wide smile on his face. He was wearing a nice, black silk button up shirt and a matching black tie. He looked very formal and very handsome. "Please come sit down," he said as he stood up.

I walked to him, and he pushed in my chair behind me. "Thank you," I said, surprised at this sudden attitude change.

He took his seat beside mine and smiled. "I wasn't actually mad at you," he said, "It just gave me a convenient excuse to come here and get everything ready."

I smacked his arm playfully. "You made me worry for nothing? I cried," I said angrily.

He picked my hand up and kissed it. "Will you forgive me?"

I smiled. "Maybe."

He whistled and the doors opened. Waiters came in carrying trays of food. "First we will eat and then we will go to our next stop."

"Next stop?" I asked curiously.

He picked up his fork and said, "You look beautiful."

Dodging the question again. "Thank you. You look very handsome." I took a bite of my food and realized how hungry I was. I did not talk again until my plate was empty and my stomach was full.

He put a wad of cash on the table and took my hand, helping me up. "Ready?"

"Where did you get all that money?" I asked, incredibly shocked. I knew he was a vice president of a business, but that was a lot of money to throw at one dinner.

"Later," he said.

I let him lead me out of the restaurant and down to the pier that overlooked the river. The sun was setting and it looked beautiful. "It's gorgeous," I whispered.

He whispered, "Yes, you are."

I turned around and saw him messing with his phone. "Did you take a picture of me?"

He smiled. "Yep. I needed a new background for my phone."

I walked to him and put my hands on his chest. "Does that mean I can get a new picture for mine as well?"

He smirked. "Of course."

I stood up on my tip toes and kissed his lips softly. He kissed me back and wrapped his arms around my waist. "You promise you're not mad at me?" I asked.

He laughed and nuzzled my neck. "Yes. I promise."

I turned around and leaned back against him as we looked out over the river. "I wish this moment would never end."

"I don't," he said, stepping back from me. I turned around and he was on one knee, holding out a ring box. "I know we haven't known each other that long, but I know you are the one I want to be with for the rest of my life. You are the perfect mate for me, strong, beautiful and smart. Now that you are in my life, I cannot imagine life without you."

Was this really happening?

"Ainsley, will you marry me?" he asked, opening the box and revealing a gorgeous diamond ring.

I walked forward, drawn by the bright diamonds gleaming at me. "Yes."

He stood up and slipped the ring on my finger and then kissed me. "I love you," he whispered.

I looked up at him and knew that it did not matter what anyone else thought or if it was too quickly for humans that we had decided to be together, it was true and he needed to hear it. "I love you, too. So, why do you have so much money?"

He laughed and kissed me again before answering. "I told you I am the vice president of my uncle's business, which my father was as well. When he died he left me a large amount of money."

My mouth dropped open. "Why didn't you tell me before?" I asked.

"I didn't want the fact that I was rich to impact your decision to marry me and be my mate," he admitted.

"I wouldn't care if you were poor," I told him. "Although I am glad that you are not going to be a small-town mechanic."

"What?" he asked.

"That was Iagan's dream."

"Not much of a dream," Ethan said with a shake of his head. "No wonder it was such an easy choice for you to pick me."

"Don't be rude," I said, pinching his arm.

"So, when do you want to leave for our vacation?"

THE DRIVE ACROSS THE COUNTRY WAS FUN AND LET ME MEET several other lion prides. I even stopped to see my mom and meet my uncle and his pride. The flight to Rome was unbearable because of the length we were inside the plane and the fact that I knew we were flying in the air. Cats did not like to fly.

Ethan and I visited every important town and every single place I wanted to see. We took a million pictures and I bought a bunch of souvenirs for our new house. During our train rides or before bed we pulled out a map and discussed possible cities to live in. We had narrowed it down to six options as we sat in our hotel room in Paris.

"Can we get a two-story house?" I asked him.

"We can get whatever you want," he said as he nuzzled my neck. "As long as it is under one million dollars."

"One million? Are you serious?" I asked in shock.

"Yeah, I think that is a reasonable amount, not too much and not too little," he said. "This is going to be the house that we start our own pride in," he reminded me. "It needs to be at least five bedrooms."

"No kid talk yet," I said seriously. "Can we put that off until my mid-twenties? Please?" I didn't want to think about kids until I was sure that he was my only mate. If I ended up taking on additional mates, kid talk would be another matter altogether.

He laughed and kissed my head. "Sure."

We talked more and then went to sleep. After another five days in France, we went to London and spent another three there. I wanted to go to Scotland and Ireland, too, so we went there as well and stayed in a few castles.

It was the greatest time of my life and I was with the greatest male. Was it possible that there were other males as wonderful as him? Others I would love as much as him?

I wasn't certain, but for now I would enjoy the time we had alone together.

AFTERWORD

Thank you for reading LONELY LIONESS. If you enjoyed the book, please consider leaving a review at your favorite book retailer.

Be on the lookout for book two in The Lioness's Harem Series where Ainsley's story continues and her harem will grow!

CONNECT WITH CATHERINE BANKS

I really appreciate you reading my book! Here are some ways to connect with me:
www.catherinebanks.com

Follow me on BookBub: https://www.bookbub.com/authors/catherine-banks

Join my newsletter for deals and snippets: http://catbanks.co/newsletter

Like my author Facebook page: http://www.Facebook.com/CatherineBanksAuthor

Follow me on Twitter: http://www.Twitter.com/catherineebanks

Follow me on Goodreads: http://www.Goodreads.com/catherine_banks

www.Turbokitten.us
www.Turbokitten.us/catherine-banks

Purchase items handmade by Catherine: http://Etsy.com/
shop/TurboKittenInd

ABOUT THE AUTHOR

Catherine Banks is a USA Today bestselling fantasy author who writes in several fantasy subgenres under two pseudonyms. She began writing fiction at only four years old and finished her first full-length novel at the age of fifteen. She is married to her soulmate and best friend, Avery, who she has two amazing children with. After her full-time job, she reads books, plays video games, and watches anime shows and movies with her family to relax. Although she has lived in Northern California her entire life, she dreams of traveling around the world. Catherine is also C.E.O. of Turbo Kitten Industries™, a company with many hats including being a book publisher and Etsy store full of nerdy fun.

facebook.com/catherinebanksauthor

twitter.com/catherineebanks

amazon.com/author/catherinebanks

bookbub.com/authors/catherine-banks

MORE FROM CATHERINE BANKS

Calvin's Alien Adventure

Pirate Princess Trilogy
Pirate Princess
Princess Triumvirate
Pirate Queen*

Little Death Bringer Duology
Mercenary
Protector
Little Death Bringer, The Official Coloring Book

Her Royal Harem Series
Royally Entangled
Royally Exposed
Royally Elected
Royally Enraged
Her Royal Harem, The Complete Series
The Demon's Fair
Her Royal Harem, The Coloring Book

Zodiac Shifters Paranormal Romance Series

Centaur's Prize

Tiger Tears

Lion About

The Lioness's Harem Trilogy

Lonely Lioness

Anderelle: Minloa Trilogy

Queen of the Stars

Empress of the Galaxy

Goddess of the Universe*

Demonic Contract

Anja's Secret

Daughter of Lions

Dragon's Blood

The Last Werewolf

Last Ama Princess

Transforming Rose

Lady Serra and the Draconian

Alys of Asgard

Phoenix Possessed

Sybil Deceived

The Pawn

Stone Heart

Of Sky and Sea

*COMING SOON